ISBN: 978-1-949621-16-7

COVE OF SANCTUARY

KEEPER OF DRAGONS BOOK 5

J.A. CULICAN

CONTENTS

To my nieces-may you always believe in dragons.

CHAPTER 1

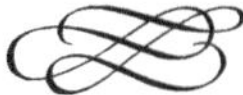

Held aloft on leathery wings, I banked left at near supersonic speed. At our altitude, the air chilled even my young dragon bones as I conserved most of my Mahier to still the air from flying so fast for the last hour. My company, a wing of Wolands spread out behind me in a "V" formation, struggled to keep up.

Shielding my grumbling thoughts was perhaps less draining than keeping the air bubble around me still, but it was no less important. The red Dragons in my wing might have frowned upon the fact that this patrol had been a spontaneous decision—meaning that I had never asked for permission to take them flying.

Still, how else could I have gotten the experience I needed? So far, tedious training with swords or marching around the flying city had been the only tasks in which I'd been authorized to lead "my" Red Dragon Wing. It was out of frustration that I'd earlier decided it would be easier to ask for forgiveness than permission.

A tingle in the back of my mind dragged me from my thoughts as another Dragon's thoughts connected with mine. *With respect, Prince Colton, is this necessary?*

I recognized the tenor in that thought-voice. Archara, of course. Arch, as the others called her, had just projected her thoughts, but not directly to me. No, she'd broadcast that to the whole wing. Just great.

That realization broke what remained of my concentration. My Dragonsight shriveled away, leaving me with nothing more than my Dragon's natural eyes—keen as a hawk's, but without magic to magnify the view, I saw only an endless sheet of Greenlandic snow almost five miles below us.

I grit my fangs. *We're practicing flying in a group. This is a new wing—new to me, at least—so I don't yet know each of you well enough to lead you effectively in battle.*

Ain't that the truth. Arch's thought slipped through her private shield, or more likely, she'd let it slip intentionally. Then, she broadcast to all of us, *These drills wouldn't have more to do with Eva and Cairo being gone, would it? If so, may I respectfully suggest that you won't bring them back from Paraiso any sooner by pointless, endless patrols?*

I ignored the jab and refocused my Mahier to magnify my view again. That done, I returned my gaze to the land below. We were on patrol, after all, ostensibly looking for any danger to Ochana flying around, as unlikely as that was. Arch mentioning my friends' departure to the Elven realm did nothing to help my mood, either. I no longer felt any urge to chatter, so having an actual job to do was a real relief.

She had a point about all this patrolling and drilling, though. It didn't take my mind off my missing companions. The last six months, however, were merely the blink of an eye to Dragonkind. Though patrolling had helped to alleviate the worst of my loneliness, it still wasn't the real reason for our patrol.

In truth, I was keenly aware that I had much to learn about leading Dragons, and as Jericho had so often said, experience was the best teacher. The fearsome old general wasn't wrong about that.

I drifted into daydreaming my friends had come home, and we were talking about my leadership progress, or rather, my lack thereof.

After a while, a deep, bassy thought-voice I recognized as Valum's whispered inside my head, *We've been flying for hours, Prince. Drake Osimon wouldn't have driven us this hard. We have no enemies left, no missions to conduct... thanks to you, of course.*

The last part felt rather grudging, as had his calling Osimon their Drake, but I left it alone. I could understand why they didn't appreciate an interloper like me taking over their wing, and I even agreed that Osimon's redeployment to make room for me had been totally unfair. Osimon, their Drake before I came along, was a Woland of high repute, a respected red Dragon warrior who had led the wing since before I was born. I had overheard much grumbling from my wing-mates since I'd been given his position a few weeks ago, and their complaints told me Osimon had not been fond of pointless patrols.

These patrols were kind of pointless... After all, we were hardly the first Dragons to fly over Greenland that day. But again, I had little choice in the matter. I needed field time with my soldiers since it didn't look like I'd get to go adventuring again any time soon, but I still felt bitter about their resentments.

That bitterness was why I snapped back at Valum, *this was King Rylan's doing, not mine, and we all have our orders—even Osimon and me. Keepers are not above the law.*

As soon as I said it, I felt the irony of talking about privilege not applying here as I flew my wing without permission in full knowledge that the worst, I'd likely suffer was my dad's private reprimand over dinner, presuming the king did even that.

Valum replied, *Between the two of us, I know this wasn't your fault. It's just that, although you may be the* Keeper of Dragons, *our wingleader trained us, and he was among the best Drakes I've served under in centuries. Now, we just have...*

The thought trailed off, but I could guess how it ended. Now, they just had... me.

I spared a moment to wish my father had ordered me

to take one of the wings he'd newly formed since my friends and I had defeated the dark Elf, King Eldrick, and his Eldren followers. My recent assignment in Osimon's place had been unfair to both the wing and its former Drake—and it wasn't fair to me, either. I flew on in silence.

Below, near the island's interior, my enhanced eyes caught sight of something streaking through the air toward the west coast at blinding speed. Probably just a human airliner, but I concentrated on seeing it up close anyway.

Its leathery wings flapped.

That was no airplane. I sent the thought out, *Contact bearing one o'clock at half-span below horizon, heading due west. All eyes, what is that?*

Arch had the keenest eyes in our wing, so I wasn't surprised when she replied first, *It's a dragon.*

I felt hot smoke trickle from my snout. *Yeah, that's what I see.*

But...

I continued for her, *But Dragons no longer live in Greenland's interior.*

She broadcast, *I think it's a Sien, Keeper, wherever it lives.*

The other Dragons' projected their agreement.

I channeled more Mahier, using Dragon magic on the distant flier to magnify it further still. At first, I thought it was a silver Dragon, too. Then, I realized it didn't glint in direct sunlight as a Sien should.

Was it... white? I had never heard of white Dragons. It couldn't have been white, could it?

Arch replied, *It sure looks white, now that you mention it.*

I hadn't realized I'd thought that out loud. I took a deep breath and gathered my magic for a moment, then focused on sending my thoughts to the unknown flier. Even at that great distance, it wasn't difficult to project them so tightly. *Hail, Dragon. This is Jameson Wing of Ochana. Please identify yourself.*

Nothing back, no thoughts, not even a ripple. I knew it heard me, though, when the strange Dragon veered right, diving straight into a cloud bank, where it vanished.

I led my patrol wing in a grid-pattern search, but we found no trace of the strange, white Dragon, not even the tell-tale wake of disturbed air where it had been. Smoothing such a subtle a sign of its passing must have used a tremendous amount of Mahier—more than most Wolands could have gathered, much less used in so short a time.

I considered the possibility that we'd just seen an agent of Ochana on some mission. It would have explained the stranger hiding from us. But if it were, then Jericho would know about it, and he'd tell me if I asked directly. Sure, he'd yell at me for being out on an unauthorized patrol, first, but I had to do it. I had to be sure.

I released a stomach-full of brimstone smoke through my snout as I circled to head back the way we had come, then straightened out to fly just as fast as my wing could follow me.

An hour later, Ochana's majestic mountain loomed into view, emerging from the clouds surrounding it. As always, its endless waterfall cast a rainbow, like a banner welcoming us home.

CHAPTER 2

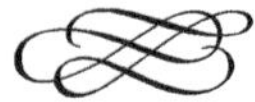

Toward the sun we flew, skimming the river's surface as it plummeted over Ochana's edge from the floating city's majestic mountain. I folded my wings back, and gravity's iron fist once again clutched us. Jealous of our flight, it pulled, bringing us inexorably down, plummeting toward Ochana's landing platforms lining its western edge.

Very poetic, Prince. Arch's tenor voice reverberated in my head...

Just before impact, I stretched my wings to catch the air like a parachute and drifted down the last couple of feet as a leaf falling from an autumn tree. *The contrast to merely falling is a delicious irony,* I replied, baring rows of fangs as my scaly lips pulled back into a Dragon's grin.

My Dragon had far sharper senses than my Human,

though, and I caught an acrid scent of burning plastic at almost the same moment my ears picked up snips of angry, raised voices. I looked around, but everything seemed okay, at least in the landing district. I noted that others were also raising ears and noses to the wind, testing it.

Shifting into my human form, the smells and sounds immediately disappeared, my senses no longer up to the task. I turned to a passing Leslo and grabbed his arm. The man wore the usual emerald-trimmed sash of a green Dragon, but it had been adorned with glittering diamond dust, so I knew he was someone important. All the green Dragons were.

I said evenly, "What's going on? My Dragon smelled fire when we landed."

But he only shrugged. "Prince Colton, my apologies, but I don't know. I caught a whiff, nothing more, with my Human nose. Your guess is as good as mine."

Our floating city's winds, constantly changing, again shifted, this time blowing gently toward us from the east. My Human nose had no problem smelling the unmistakable odor the breeze carried, and presently, a faint haze appeared.

"Something's burning," Aurara said, again in her Human, "and it's not Dragonfire."

Valum, still in his Dragon, growled identifiable words with a heavy lisp. "So tired... Can't launch to see. Hear... fighting?" He pointed the tip of his tail over his shoulder, toward the east.

"We're all tired." I waved at my landing wing. "Summon

your humans, Jameson Wing, and follow me. I know you're exhausted, but we soldiers only get to be tired on our own time."

I strode down the steps to the boulevard that ran parallel to the landing platforms, crossed the street, and walked briskly down an intersecting street that ran east to west. As we marched east in formation, my exhaustion made it hard to keep my head up, but we had a duty, and being tired from one idiot wingleader's illicit patrol didn't excuse us from it.

As we continued, I spotted other Wolands also maneuvering through the growing crowd as they headed in the same general direction. I also heard angry, shouting voices becoming clearer and louder with each stride. I found my wingmates moving almost elbow-to-elbow with me, though I'd not ordered any formation, and their close presence was a relief. Their anxiety, on the other hand, made me all the more wary. I trusted their instincts more than my own, but this time, theirs matched mine.

Abruptly, someone grabbed my arm. I looked down to find a mailed glove gripping me, and followed the arm up to see it was worn by a green Dragon. This one's emerald sash was trimmed in silver, perhaps some kind of administrator.

"Prince, thank Aprella you're here. You have to stop this! There's fighting going on all through a small Galian neighborhood. People are going to get hurt."

I tried to smile reassuringly, though keeping my eyes from darting all over the place was a test of willpower. I managed it, somehow. "Of course, I will. Can you tell me why they're fighting?"

He let go of my arm. "We don't yet know, but it's bigger than the others. We've got bucket brigades standing by, and others putting out a house fire, but I'm afraid it won't be enough if the Galians start to light it all up and burn it down."

"Why would they burn down their own neighborhood?" And why the blue Dragons? Galians were Ochana's nurturers, not fighters.

I got no answer, though, as the Leslo sprinted ahead. I nodded to my wing and then continued on, setting a brisk pace. Answers would come soon enough.

Approaching the Galian neighborhood, I began to note silver and green Dragons running from the riotous neighborhood. By the time I crossed the street and saw the numerous Wolands standing around, waiting for directions, there were just as many greens and silvers staring at the scene before them, most with shock etched on their faces.

I parted a squad of Wolands in red service armor, and when I got a clear view, I stopped to stare, shocked like the onlookers. Lining both sides of the street bisecting the rioting blocks, dozens of Galians stood with fists in the air, chanting something I couldn't understand. With so many voices shouting it out of unison, it was just a rumbling, deep roar. I immediately noted that more Galians were standing at the intersection, filling it from corner to corner and beyond, down the intersection's side roads, until the mob stretched out of view.

Dozens of enraged Galians were shouting at the Woland perimeter hemming them in, and pockets of fighting had broken out. There were a few skirmishes between blue Galians, but there were some silver Siens as well. The maelstrom was barely contained by red Dragons in various states of armor all around the four-block neighborhood's outer edge, struggling to stand their ground in the face of an even greater number of Galians trying to shove their way through.

Rocks flew through the air, peppering some of the soldiers, and one landed only a foot or two from my feet. I looked up again to find a green Dragon standing behind the thin line of armored Wolands, looking at me. She pointed into the Galian neighborhood.

"Prince Colton, at last. Do you see this mayhem?"

"Yes, I—"

The Leslo continued, shouting over me, "For Aprella's sake, do something. Do you see what they're doing to their own neighborhood?"

I nodded, looking back into the chaos. "It's impossible to miss."

"The reds won't listen to me. You have to send them in! There are Siens in danger in there, but these guardians are only keeping this from spreading. What about the ones inside?"

"I won't go in with warriors against those who are

normally our gentlest race, not without a good understanding of what's going on. What exactly is 'this' that's spreading?" I glared at the Leslo, who stared back at me with wide, disbelieving eyes.

A Woland stepped up beside me with his co-wing in a semicircle behind him. "Prince Colton, you know as much as we do, but I say it's high time these greedy Galians stop asking for more. And more, and more. Pushy damned blues, always trying to take what rightly belongs to others. Ochana doesn't have the resources to give them everything they feel entitled to." He spit on the pavement, nose wrinkled in disgust.

Valum stepped up beside the soldier and growled at me, his eyes glowing red for a moment. "The Leslos and Wolands need to put these traitors in their place, Keeper. The damnable Siens in there, too. Duke Sepens was right all along."

"About what?" I looked back and forth between Valum and the mob, itching to do something, anything, but the wrong move could turn this into a full-blown riot.

"Wolands and Leslos need a fair share, too, but Aprella damn them, these Galians dare to demand more. That comes from someone else's share, Keeper."

I was about to ask who the Sepens were, but Arch grabbed his arm and growled at him. "Valum, don't you dare start spouting that Sepens nonsense."

"Are you saying they don't take more than their share?" He watched her warily, eyes narrowed.

Arch made a *tsk* sound, sucking her teeth. She looked right back into his eyes. "Aprella only knows where you heard that nonsense, but Valum, we're *protectors*, not tyrants. We took an oath, and while we Wolands might do most of the bleeding for all the races of Truth, do you really think we could do *our* duty without those Galians doing what *they* do?"

Valum looked down, gritting his teeth. "A warrior is honest. No, we could not."

She clapped him on the shoulder, warrior to warrior, though her eyes locked with mine and she pressed her lips together, little wrinkles appearing at the corners. She looked as worried as I felt.

Another Woland from my wing let out a hiss, smoke tendrils rising from his nostrils. "Bah. The old king would never have allowed this greed to fester into... whatever *this* nonsense is. They think they beat Eldrick with their own hands. It's stupid. Permission to go do my job, sir?"

I nodded, and he stormed away to the line of warriors barricading the riot in.

My stomach churned. What on Earth was going on? The war had ended six months ago, and for six months, I'd been in Ochana. I said to Arch, "This is the first time I've seen anything like this, or even heard such dissent among the Dragon races—"

To my right, a commotion interrupted me, and a woman at least several centuries old was struggling against the

Wolands' barricading arms. "Prince Colton," she called, jumping up and reaching toward me.

I approached, looking at her directly. I expected to see anger in those eyes, and I wasn't prepared for the despair I saw instead. I waited for her to say something else, something to explain all of this, but a moment later, her sad eyes flared with blue light.

The Wolands shoved her back, hard.

I only watched, unsure what to do.

The shove made her stagger and fall backward. Instinctively, I took a step toward her, but there was little I could do about it without pushing through the Wolands to wade into that chaos.

She climbed to her feet, holding her arm, and shouted at me, "You see this? Keeper of Dragons—bah! You're a disappointment, Prince."

"Silence, woman," a Woland growled at her. "That's 'Prince Colton' to the likes of you, Galian."

Tears on her cheeks, she glared at me and shoved her fist in the air, showing the anger I'd expected earlier. "You stand for more than just the old ways, Keeper. I thought you stood for all of us."

A moment later, she was lost to the crowd of chanting, angry blue Dragons, but her words echoed in my ears.

CHAPTER 3

Ever more Wolands showed up at the riot, and they organized themselves into squads. Though many reinforced the perimeter around the riot, a veritable army of red Dragons gathered, formed up, and produced shields and batons. I considered stopping them, but they had a duty to perform. I let them and watched helplessly as they waded into the crowd, swinging their weapons. Watching them break up the chaos was hard, but maybe it had to be done. This was a riot, not a discussion, and that was no way to voice grievances—especially not how the nurturing, blue Galians ought to. It looked to me like half the buildings in there were on fire.

For maybe half an hour, I watched the melee, and I was surprised to discover there were more than a few Siens in there, as well, shouting alongside the blues. I was glad the soldiers didn't use swords, but I was rather surprised that so many carried bludgeons.

The crowd began to give way before the disciplined march of armored soldiers. The strategy came as no surprise, though. Wolands were soldiers, not nurturers, and even using blunt instruments, they left more than a few injured Galians in their wake. The wounded were left lying on sidewalks and streets, some trying to crawl away. Others seemed unable to move and just cried out for help.

That was about the time vehicles approached from the west in a line, but they weren't just cars. The few cars in Ochana were nothing like human cars, but the vehicles snaking their way toward us, I recognized. Red ambulances pulled up to the cordon, and I breathed a sigh of relief. Help for the wounded had finally arrived.

When the doors opened, though, the people who climbed out didn't wear silver-trimmed sashes and paramedic uniforms as I'd expected. They wore red armor, instead, and carried swords or spears. Real weapons. That's when I noticed the ambulances didn't have white crosses on their sides, and the cab windows were crisscrossed by thin bars. Thicker bars covered the small side windows.

I turned to Arch, my pulse racing. "I didn't know soldiers managed the ambulances."

She shrugged, glancing at Valum.

He raised an eyebrow at me. "Our ambulances are blue, Keeper. Those are transports."

"Transports to where, exactly?" I looked him in the eyes, already knowing the answer.

"Jail, for processing and holding, I imagine."

I ran to the nearest transport and stepped between the driver and the barricade. "You'll take me with you."

He stopped and stared a moment, then bowed slightly with his left fist over his chest. "Of course, Prince, but you don't need to concern yourself with this rabble. I promise you, they'll get what they deserve for this."

"And does that include medical treatment for all those hurt people in there?" A trail of smoke curled up around my nose, and I fought to calm myself.

"I'm sure they'll be treated, once they're processed—those who deserve it, at least."

I resisted the urge to grab the soldier's shirt and shake him. He was just following someone's orders, and making a scene wouldn't help anyone or change the situation in any way. So, I nodded, instead, and held my hand out toward the barricade soldiers.

"Very well, then. I won't keep you from your duty any longer. But those are Dragons in there. Remember that."

I stood aside, watching the red Dragons as they handcuffed many of the Galians they'd either caught running or who hadn't been able to flee in time. As they worked, I stayed conspicuously visible in hopes that my mere presence helped to keep the wounded safe. No one was going to get hurt further en route, not while I was around.

I dismissed my wing as the last captured Galians were loaded into the transports, and a Woland guard volunteered to fly to the facility so I could ride in his place. I made a note of his name before he left so I could commend him for that.

Soon, we arrived at Ochana's jail center. I had never seen it before except from a distance, but as it turned out, it wasn't much to look at. A two-story building formed a square that covered half a block, with three-story watchtowers at the corners. It looked pretty much as I'd expected a jail to look.

The transports pulled up along the curb, and the Wolands began to herd prisoners inside. They ordered the healthy prisoners to carry in those few who couldn't walk.

The jail's interior was quieter than I'd expected as uniformed soldiers went about their duties efficiently. I found the Woland who looked like he was in charge, an older man who nonetheless was still rather burly, and I waved away his startled salute.

"Never mind that," I said. "There are injured Dragons among the prisoners."

"Yes." He raised one eyebrow. "I see that. If you don't mind, sir, I have a job to do. It's going to be a long night for us."

I took a deep breath, fighting my rising outrage. He was only doing his job, just as the transport teams had been. I merely had an issue with that job, at least at this exact moment.

"Why weren't the wounded taken to receive medical attention, before taking them here?"

He looked at his wrist, where he wore a sturdy-looking digital watch, as unusual in Ochana as it was down on Earth these days. "The Leslos are sending a judge first thing in the morning, and that's only a few hours away."

"So, they sit here bleeding until then?"

"I understand your concern, but none of these rioters are hurt badly enough to perish before then, and we have a Galian healer on duty at all times to handle any surprises, among them or our other inmates."

I took a deep breath, nodding.

He added, "But these Galians... Prince Colton, they *rioted*. They dared demand more than their share, and they already *get* more than their share. They're disloyal at best, and I'm sure you have more important things to do than babysit a bunch of— "

"Don't tell me my duty," I said, cutting him off. "These Galians are my duty every bit as much as you and every other Dragon in Ochana. I do not only protect the ones who agree with me. Now, I want..."

I trailed off as the door opened again, and I saw a familiar pair of red, glowing eyes set above a nose already trailing a hefty cloud of angry smoke. Somehow, Jericho always seemed to be about ready to tear someone's head off. Usually, mine.

I took a deep breath and readied myself for whatever the general would scream at me for doing wrong this time.

"Prince Cole." He walked up to me, ignoring the jailer who glanced appreciatively at him before scurrying off to get back to work.

I saluted, fist over chest. As the crown prince, I didn't have to, but as a soldier in his chain of command, I'd always just felt it was appropriate, especially in front of others. "Jericho. Why are you here, General?"

He nodded, mouth ticking upward at the corners as I saluted. "I heard you were here, and I came to ask you that very same question. Do you mind telling me why the Prince of Ochana is here bothering my jailer, yelling at my soldiers, and generally not being where he's supposed to be?"

"They're Ochana's soldiers." I met his gaze, my heart beating faster. It wasn't the first time I'd challenged his view of how things should run, and likely wouldn't be the last, but it was always a nerve-wracking decision. Jericho was big, far bigger than me, and I had no doubt who'd win a fight. Thankfully, I was pretty sure he wasn't going to get in a fight with the king's son—not in front of so many witnesses.

"Yes, they're Ochana's soldiers. As am I, Cole. You're Ochana's soldier, too. So tell, me, soldier, why are you here messing with other soldiers doing their jobs instead of keeping your own wing under control? For Aprella's sake, you're the *prince,* and you can't control five highly trained Wolands?"

What? I blinked at him. As his words sunk in, though,

my shock slipped away. Righteous indignation aptly described the feeling that took its place. "You think I didn't have my wing under control, is that it?"

"That's what I said. Why, Cole, did you not have your wing, which I personally put under you, under control?"

"When was this? Be specific, because I have no idea what you're talking about, sir," I heard myself snap back and wished I could stop the words coming out of my mouth. I kept going, almost hoping I could just out-talk him and he'd leave. "I don't know why you think my team wasn't under control, General, but I do know one thing."

"Oh? Do tell." He looked me in the eyes, his mouth turning up a tiny bit more at one corner.

"What I know is that if you never leave me alone with my team and keep second-guessing everything I do, they'll never learn to trust me. You and Dad stuck me with a tight unit, yanking their far more capable leader unfairly, and then you expect them to respect the king's snot-nosed kid? And *then,* you come along and undermine me every chance you get. And—"

Jericho held up one hand as his half-smile faded. "Enough. This is neither the time nor the place for this. But don't you ever call yourself a snot-nosed kid again where I can hear you, or I'm going to take you out back and tan you like one. You're a prince, and the Keeper of Dragons. Aprella knows why, but the Fates gave us you—and *you* did what no one else could. *You* saved the world. *You* had better start acting like it, because I promise you, every person in every race of Truth knows what you don't seem to know."

"I—"

"Negative." He leaned forward until his face hovered six inches from mine. "No arguments, Cole. Go home. Get sleep. Tomorrow is another day, and I expect you out there training them. Go on patrol. Work the swords. Whatever. Just do something productive."

"I... Yes, sir, but..."

"Cole, if you were anyone else, I'd strip your rank so fast your head would spin. Not for stupidly going out on patrol with no one knowing where the Crown Prince of Ochana had gone, but because your lack of confidence is toxic."

"So, why don't you, then? My wing could go back to having a wingleader they respect instead of me."

"Because I know what kind of man you are, even if you don't seem to know it yourself. Because as unsure of yourself as you can be, you don't run from danger. You don't shrink from duty. And you aren't afraid to stand up to me, even if it drives me crazy half the time. Now go home, Cole. Go sleep, but first, eat a cow. That's an order."

His eyes flared brighter still, and smoke came from both nostrils. His left eye twitched as we stared at one another.

Suddenly, the heat left me, and I became aware of a dozen people watching us. Any outburst I made now would be retold far and wide by the time any judge arrived in a few hours. I spun on my heels and tried to hold my head as high as I could as I walked out, feeling every one of those gazes boring into my back. I let the doors slam.

The moment I turned the corner out of view from the jail lobby, I started to run. Faster and faster, I kept running. It was a release of sorts, and I soon entered a kind of trance from the hypnotic rhythm of my boots pounding on pavement.

As my thoughts spun all sorts of things I *should* have said but hadn't thought of, my feet took me home on their own accord, running the whole way. I only slowed when I finally approached the castle gates, and I headed to bed without even stopping by the kitchen for a cow's worth of steaks.

But when I got to my room, despite my exhaustion from flying all those hours and the riot afterward, my mind wouldn't shut up. My thoughts wouldn't leave me alone. No matter how many juicy sheep I counted in my head, my thoughts stayed stubbornly fixed on the Galians, their riot, and the manner in which they'd been treated after soldiers broke it up. Jericho's odd statement about my lack of confidence also danced in my head, refusing to shut up.

Sleep was a long time in coming.

I reduced the Mahier I pumped into my bubble, allowing myself to feel some of the wind beneath my wings as I led my wing soaring over Greenland. This time, not only were we not violating orders—unbeknownst to my soldiers—I had Jericho's personal authorization. His orders, more like. At least my temper tantrum of the night before had born fruit, which reduced my sting of embarrassment about the whole thing, if only a tiny bit.

I broadcast to my wing, *Echelon-left, on my mark.*

When I gave the go-ahead to execute the order, the right arm of Dragons trailing me in V-formation shifted left, while the dragons on the left spaced out to make room. The two arms merged like a zipper, until all five Dragons had spread behind me and to my left. Textbook perfect.

Evasion protocol. I veered right, and the five others each broke in a different direction. Up, down, diagonal... It was also a textbook maneuver.

Ten seconds later, they were again in left-echelon formation behind me. I was about to order echelon-up, ideal for strafing a troop column on the ground, when I spotted movement in the clouds below me.

I pumped Mahier to my eyes, my Dragonsight magnifying to get a better view, and right away, I saw it was the white dragon. I almost let the thought slip in my excitement.

Circle in a holding pattern. Do it now, I broadcast to my wing, then folded my wings.

My path arched downward, and a moment later, I was streaking like a hawk diving for prey. At about 200 meters, I extended my wings to arrest my plummet and match the white dragon's course and speed.

Clearing my mind, I broadcast to the white, *do not attempt to evade, by the authority of Jameson Wing, Ochana. Do you understand?*

As seconds ticked by, I expected the dragon to try to escape, but then the dragon replied in a woman's voice, her fear as evident as if I'd felt it myself, *I hear and I obey.*

I accelerated and dropped lower until I was just above and behind her on the right. *Identify yourself, please.*

I heard a mental sigh. She didn't even try to block it. *I'm Arden Sepens. I didn't know flying over Greenland was against the rules. I'm new to Ochana. How much trouble am I really in?*

I didn't let Arden hear my chuckle. A new Dragon... I vividly remembered my own awkward first days, after all, so I replied, *You're not in trouble. It's our duty to contact anyone we see in Ochana's airspace and report it. It's nothing more.*

Instantly, she radiated fear.

Alarm bells went off in my head. What was she hiding?

I'm not hiding anything, came her instant reply, though I hadn't realized I'd let that question slip out. *I don't even want to be here. I was just fine where I was, with my human family.*

A Dragon's frown involves baring our fang-like teeth, so I was glad she wasn't in position to see my expression as I replied, *then why hide your presence out here?*

I... I'm not really allowed to leave the family estate, yet. I don't know why. But I can't sit in my room and stare at the walls anymore. I needed to burn off my frustration, and nothing does it like a marathon flight.

Well, that was understandable. I'd just ran off my own

frustrations the night before, after all. I let my empathy leak through my mental shield, hoping to calm her.

She replied, *You're the first person I've met outside my own family here. Can't you please just maybe cut me a break? Just keep me out of your report. Please?*

I was probably going to end up in trouble over this, but she wasn't really breaking any rules, and family obligations were a burden I could sympathize with. I'd just have to keep my mental shield up when I got back to my wing…

My wing! I'd forgotten I left them in a holding pattern. They'd come looking soon, I was certain. *Time to cut this short. I'll tell you what—we can keep this out of our report if you return to Ochana and stop breaking your family's rules. I don't think we need to get you in trouble, but the next wing you encounter may not be so understanding. Are we clear?*

Arden gave me a mental image of a human hand making the thumbs-up gesture, and she veered away. *Thanks, protector. I hope we meet again. I'll stay where I'm supposed to be from now on.*

I watched as she accelerated toward Ochana. Somehow, I doubted she was going to stay locked in her room, but maybe she'd be more careful the next time. I only hoped my decision wouldn't get me yelled at again.

Hah. Jericho would find some other reason to yell, no doubt.

I banked away and headed back to my waiting wing, pouring more Mahier into my mental shields along the way.

CHAPTER 4

In the morning, I found my schedule was blessedly empty. Well, it said "reserved," but whatever it was reserved for, it wasn't patrols or drills. Good enough.

I closed the hologram displaying the day's schedule, wiping my hand over the projector node built into the table, and carefully returned my daily-wear armor to its mannequin before tossing on a pair of jeans and a hoodie.

I had just slid the black fabric over my head when someone knocked on my door. Pulling the hoodie down and smoothing it as I walked to the door, I dismissed the Mahier with which I'd locked it and opened the door.

An ornately dressed Dragon stood almost at attention, like a soldier, but his nose was a lot higher in the air. A Leslo, judging by the trim around his silk sash. "Prince

Colton, good morning. The Ochana Council requests the honor of your presence this morning. I believe you found your schedule had been cleared?"

I nodded. Seeing the council wasn't what I had in mind, but I hadn't seen Councilors Allas, Jules, and Luka since the Time of Fear. I smiled at the thought. "Okay. Right now?"

"Indeed, sir. However, I might suggest more appropriate... attire." His nose wrinkled at my jeans and hoodie outfit.

I let out a sigh and closed the door. Neither the councilors nor the king would care if I wore jeans, but I still pulled out my official costume—not the most formal one, but the next one down. It was a small protest but not so blatant that anyone could rebuke me for it. I hoped it irritated the envoy outside, though, and smiled at the thought.

Once dressed, I opened the door again, and the envoy's roving eyes shouted disapproval. "Very well, sir. I shall escort you presently."

"Verily, thee and thy charge canst bounceth." I grinned, but he just spun on his heels and marched down the hallway, nose up high.

"No sense of humor." I sighed, then followed him with my hands in my pockets.

The envoy announced my presence formally. This had never

been not awkward for me, and every head in the council chamber swiveled our way. King Rylan stood to one side, speaking to a couple of Dragons I didn't recognize, and a trio of everything but Wolands stood off to the other side. I didn't see the councilors, though.

King Rylan smiled and raised his hand. "There's my boy. Cole, come over here. Let me introduce you to a family you haven't yet met."

I approached, casually scanning the two green Dragons with him. Their sashes were trimmed in emerald green, meaning they were Leslos like my father. But where the king's and my sashes bore an identical embroidered pattern, the newcomers' sashes were only the same at first glance. After a moment, I spotted subtle differences between theirs and ours.

The younger one was tall, strong, and his gaze was uncomfortably direct. Well, he looked comfortable with it, but I wasn't. The older one was tall, like his son, but he was thinner, and he had faint wrinkles around his eyes. He didn't bother to watch me approach.

I bowed slightly, formally stiff. "Welcome to Ochana. With whom do I have the pleasure of meeting?"

Rylan replied, "This is Umbran Sepens and his son, Trey. Theirs is a family as old and respected as ours, son. They're also kin, albeit distant."

Umbran narrowed his eyes at my father but didn't look my way. "A pleasure, I'm sure."

Trey, who did look at me, smiled wanly. "A pleasure

indeed. So, this is the mighty Keeper of Dragons. We hear so much about you these days. They say you had quite the streak of luck in defeating the Eldrens. We Leslos have all the luck, am I right? Better to be lucky than good, I suppose."

I glanced at Rylan, but maybe he had been too busy smiling at me to notice the slight, if it had been one. I was pretty certain it had been. It wasn't worth commenting on, though.

As his son spoke, Umbran took a champagne flute from a server without so much as a nod in thanks or even a glance. How very noble. I kept that thought to myself, though.

Rylan laughed. "Luck runs out, young Sepens. My son had plenty of that, too, out there, but the Fates smiled on him. In the end, skill and Leslo grit prevailed where luck failed. A good thing, too, or we'd all be short one planet to live on."

"Hm." Umbran nodded.

Trey said, "Then you have my thanks, Prince Colton. So, how have things been going here in the Dragon realm? Any issues with the other colors? Obviously, not the Wolands, of course. Thank Aprella, we have at least one stalwart race of Dragons who know their duty, eh?"

I feigned a smile. "Nothing we can't handle. I feel like all the Dragon races are stalwart in their own way. They just aren't all great at swinging swords."

Rylan laughed, his emerald eyes lighting with mirth. "Well said. Their efforts provide our Wolands the time they need to learn how to swing those swords so well, I say."

He turned to the cluster of three Dragons and waved them over. "In any case, Cole, our relations are not the only people you need to meet."

The others approached, their silver, green, and blue-trimmed sashes a riot of clashing patterns, but each sash looked more elegant than the last.

He said, "These are councilors Xavier of Leslo, Marjorie of Sien, and Edgar of Galian. Honorable Councilors, I'm honored to present to you Prince Colton, Keeper of Dragons, protector of the Races of Truth, defender of Ochana, and all-around best son I could have asked for."

My eyes went wide. These were the councilors? "I... It is my pleasure to meet the Honorable Councilors of Ochana."

Xavier bowed his head. "The pleasure is ours."

A voice behind me said, "Cole, there you are."

I glanced over my shoulder and found a new arrival—Jericho, in full-dress Woland uniform.

He greeted the new councilors by name, though his gaze kept flicking back to me. Formalities kept, he said, "Cole, you look surprised to see me here."

I kept my expression neutral. "I hope the, uh, previous councilors are well?"

Jericho nodded. "They're fine, I'm sure. There has been a slight change of politics, that's all. You haven't yet been around long enough to see it happen before, but this actually happens pretty often. Shifting alliances change priorities, and our councilors serve Ochana as much by knowing when to step aside as they had by serving on Ochana's Council."

"I see." I didn't, really, but I could only plow ahead. "So, what shifting priorities led to these promotions? Well-earned, I'm sure," I added hastily.

Xavier inclined his head, acknowledging both the faux pas and the recovery, or so it seemed to me. "I certainly hope to earn the assignment. As to your question, it seems that we have seen fewer new Dragons than expected, of late. We track births, of course. The expected number of Dragons have shown up for recent new Dragon celebrations and orientation, but among all the Dragon races, we have been seeing fewer births than we should. Particularly in a war's aftermath, we should see more births, not fewer."

Trey cleared his throat. "Perhaps those *human* families have not been caring for our future well enough. Perhaps they aren't taking proper care of their Dragon charges."

Rylan's cheerful expression lessened, though mostly around his eyes. "We're well aware of the Sepens family's concerns, but I assure you, your concerns are unfounded. Our human caretakers continue to care well for our children. Speaking of our young ones, though, where is the youngest member of your family? Isn't she supposed to be joining us in Ochana soon?"

Umbran's eyes narrowed, the wrinkles at his eyes seeming well familiar with the expression for a moment. "How kind of you to inquire about her. Arden, my daughter, will of course come to Ochana soon. I will be delighted to introduce you when she arrives."

My eyes widened for a moment, but I hid the slip-up by running my hand through my short hair. Arden Sepens? *This* Sepens family? Theirs was a common enough surname, but Arden wasn't. I'd never met another person who shared the white Dragon's name.

And she was already in Ochana.

CHAPTER 5

From across the table, Arch raised her glass in the air. "We appreciate the night out, Prince Colton... Cole, rather. Sorry. I know you said this was an unofficial outing and not to be so formal, but it's hard to break such a deep habit."

I smiled at her. "No apology needed. And I know you all probably thought I was trying to bribe you to like me, though no one turned down a top-notch meal on the royal tab, but that didn't have anything to do with my invitation."

It would have been a nice bonus, though, if a mere dinner improved my standing as a commander. Then again, these were professional soldiers. My royal blood and endless tab didn't really matter to them.

Valum grinned. "We soldiers are creatures of habit."

"That's true everywhere, I've noticed, not only among

you Dragon soldiers, but all the races of Truth I've fought beside." I raised my glass to Arch in return.

She said, "Well, we may have habits most Leslos don't, but I hope you're getting used to them."

"A bit. Remember that I didn't even know I was a Dragon until the Time of Fear began. Oh, you were right about the food here, by the way."

Valum leaned back in his chair, sliding his plate back from the edge, which drew a few looks from the far more elegantly dressed diners nearby. "It's good, right?"

That was a bit of an understatement, actually. I nodded enthusiastically. "It's excellent. Better than the castle chefs' food, maybe, but don't tell them I said so. How did you find this place?"

Valum looked around to his four wingmates, but no one replied.

I hastily added, "I mean, I eat out all the time, but never here. That's going to change."

He grinned. "We came here for a promotion celebration for Arch's brother. It was on the army's dime, of course. This place is way outside a grunt's pay-grade. I really just suggested it to see how sincere you were when you said we could pick any place we wanted."

I paused, not sure how to respond to that. I couldn't decide if that was a jab or just a soldier's plain old truth.

Arch nudged his elbow with hers. "Val, that was rude, you ape."

He rubbed his arm, clearly exaggerating. "The truth is rude?"

"It is when you say it," she replied with a smirk.

I was there to get to know them better outside of merely barking orders, so I smiled in return. "It's fine. I don't blame you, Valum. I'm just the king's spoiled kid, right? But—"

Arch's smile vanished. "Stop. Don't say that again, Cole."

"Say what?"

"You wield Mahier, like us, but also every kind of magic I've ever heard of. But instead of taking over, you saved us all." Valum leaned forward almost imperceptibly. "And you defeated Eldrick when we couldn't. You saved the Troll race, and the Elven realm, and Ochana, too."

Arch nodded, agreeing. "Not one of us could wield the Mere Blade, but you do. Are we embarrassing you yet?"

She said that last part so nonchalantly that I almost missed it, and found myself grinning as it registered. "Yes, a bit." Best to change the subject, however. "The truth is, I didn't do any of those things. Fate did it. I was just along for the ride."

Valum took a gulp of ale, then wiped his mouth on his sleeve. "I'm pretty sure the Eldrens had their own prophecy, Cole. Even a Leslo soldier like you can put one foot in front of the other when things are hard, and you did. But you know as well as we do that the Fates' intentions were never known for sure until the end. A true soldier keeps going as long as he has breath in his lungs and blood in his heart."

"Or she does," Arch added, glaring.

Valum leaned back in his chair. "Too true. Wolands carry their weight, always. But my point is just that, although we can have issues with a new drake, we have none about you personally, Cole. Unlike those greedy Galians."

"Thanks, really." I raised my glass. "My issues with all you Wolands aren't personal, either."

Valum cocked his head, but Arch almost spit, grinning with a mouthful of ale.

Thereafter, things really did seem to lighten up between us. Time seemed to speed up a bit, which was good. I felt like a lot of tension between us drained. Maybe this was a good idea, after all, taking them out on the town. They certainly seemed nice enough, but after meeting Umbran and Trey Sepens, I wasn't too sure about anyone who thought they had a monopoly on understanding the Galians. Maybe these reds weren't such good people to know beyond commanding them, after all. Certainly, Valum had some opinions I couldn't stand.

Keeping a smile going became harder after that thought. When we stopped for snacks at a gold-plated taco truck, I paid for us all and told them I had an early meeting in the morning, and we meandered back toward the barracks.

Someone had set the evening's thermostat to pleasantly warm, and my five red Dragon soldiers happily chatted about small things as we walked back toward their barracks.

The castle was on the way, but until we got there, I smiled and laughed when it seemed appropriate, yet mostly just listened.

That turned out to be eye-opening, even though they didn't discuss the nature of life, the universe, and everything. Rather, it turned out that Wolands were just people, too, like everyone else. I was so used to thinking of them as soldiers that I'd never really stopped to consider there could be more to them than training, fighting, and more training.

They talked about books they enjoyed, the food they hated that everyone else loved, and more illuminating, they chatted about what they would do if they hadn't been soldiers. Valum was passionate about numbers, and surprisingly, he was an accomplished amateur statistician. That hulking brute loved something called risk analysis.

Arch, on the other hand, loved to garden, and until she talked about how hard it was to keep nutrients in the soil without additive fertilizers, I'd never realized she was behind the flower pots, window planters, and herb gardens around the barracks. Part of her wished she'd been born a Sien, because silver Dragons could be farmers.

Like I said, it was an eye-opener for me.

I was only half-listening to Arch talk about her favorite flower, a genetic-splice hybrid of sunflowers and carnations that produced honey-sweet sunflower seeds, when I looked around and realized where we were.

To our right, an entire city block was almost black with fire damage. Some were essentially gone. A few looked to have work crews busily demolishing condemned skeletons of what had been Galian homes only that morning.

A nudge at my elbow jerked me out of my thoughts, and I found Valum by my side, watching me intently with a raised eyebrow. He grinned, then turned to look at the neighborhood, too.

"It's easy to get lost in thought when you see a shame like this one, isn't it? Those selfish Galians. The fools burned their own homes."

"They were angry about something," I replied. "Angry enough to stand up to soldiers."

Valum shrugged. "Yeah, well. All I know is, this is why they aren't in charge. Leslos would never burn their own homes to send a message to their rightful liege."

As he spoke, a Sien came out from the nearest damaged building carrying a stack of charred two-by-four boards. He staggered, tripping on something, and ended up falling down and dropping his burden. I walked toward the Sien and held out my hand to help him up.

The soot-covered silver Dragon smiled and took my hand up. "Thanks, Prince Colton. I'm surprised—never mind."

"Surprised at what?" I gave him a faint smile. It wasn't hard to guess.

"Green Dragons don't usually help fallen silvers, sir. Especially royal ones. I shouldn't have said that, though. I'm sorry, and thank you."

I checked out my wingmates, but they merely watched me, curious.

"No need for apologies." I reached down and grabbed a few of his dropped boards. "Hold out your arms," I commanded.

He did so as a few more Siens came out with loads similar to his. I loaded the boards across his forearms, then grabbed a couple more. They were surprisingly heavy.

"I don't know how you carried these for the whole shift without draining your magic. Why haven't you grabbed more workers to help?"

He scratched his sweaty head, which gleamed under the artificial lights. "There are only six of us working this site, Prince. It's a demo job, just clearing it away so we can build new homes here."

"So few, though. It seems like the job would go faster if you paired up, at least." I set the last of his dropped lumber in his arms.

"Perhaps it seems so, sir. But would you excuse me? Our supervisor won't care who I was talking to if we don't get this done in time." He bowed low and waited.

Arch called out, "Cole, are you coming?"

I pursed my lips and took a deep breath. I was tired, it was late... I surprised myself though by calling back, "No, I'm staying to help. Go on without me, okay?"

She shrugged and started walking again. Of the other four, only Valum paused to look back and forth between his departing companions and me, hesitating. Then, he turned after the others. "Hey, wait for me."

As he left, I couldn't help but sigh. I only allowed myself a moment like that because there was work to do and workers who couldn't wait on me.

"Sir…" the Sien gently prodded me. "May I please return to my task?"

I smiled at him, pushing thoughts of my wing aside. "Of course, go on. What can I do to help, though?"

"Sir?"

I stifled a frustrated sigh. Everyone seemed to think I was a delicate flower who couldn't do anything no matter what I'd done before. "Was I unclear? I'll rephrase it, then. Is there a manner in which you would prefer I assist you in demolishing this ruined structure?"

He grinned. "This is a joke, right?"

I raised an eyebrow at him. "It's late, I have duty in the morning, and I'm not laughing. If this is a joke, the punchline is when you have to carry all this *without* my help." I smiled at the last moment and hoped he didn't feel stung by my words.

"Prince Colton, the mighty Keeper of Dragons, helping a night-worker Sien. It's not what I expected, but if you're serious, we're carrying out debris those inside are tearing down."

"Fair enough." I went to the door he had come through and stepped inside.

Like a curtain had dropped, Ochana's night light was cut

off. Everything went charcoal black until I used a sliver of Mahier to focus the light there was. In a moment, I could see clearly. Two Siens were at the back of what looked to have been a living room. They were ripping boards and slats down quickly, tossing them into a stack near the door.

I reached for the stack to grab more boards while the two rippers carried on with their work, apparently not seeing me in the darkness.

One said, "Well, I'm going for it."

Boards came free from the building's frame, and he grabbed one in each hand, looking at his partner as he turned toward the stack.

"Yeah, well, I want to see this so-called Sanctuary place with my own eyes before we make a move. After all, if we—"

He stopped, eyes wide. "Prince Cole? I... we... Good eve, Keeper. How can we be of service?"

Even in his human form, I could feel his nervousness through the sliver of Mahier that allowed me to see him clearly. He certainly had my attention. I managed a warm smile, though I wasn't even sure he could see it in the inky darkness.

"Good eve to you, as well. I was out and happened to see the other Siens working. I thought I could help out a bit, so they pointed me to your lumber pile."

"Of course, we'd be honored to have you working with us. Aprella knows, many hands make light work."

"It's a surprise, that's all. Thank you," added the first one.

"Cool. I can see there's a lot to be done and not a lot of you to do it. I'll try not to knock anything over in the process." I hefted two ten-foot boards, letting another trickle of Mahier make light work of it, and whistled softly as I maneuvered them through the doorway.

Outside, I had to let the magic fade from my eyes. It was surprising how much radiant light Ochana cast at night. As the brightness faded to a more comfortable level again, I saw a familiar Sien shifting wood in the lumber pile out front, apparently making it more stable while the remaining three Siens passed by on their way back to the doorway, all smiles.

After a couple more trips, I supposed they no longer thought I was joking about helping, because their mood seemed to have lightened significantly. There was probably a lesson in that, somewhere.

I set the boards down as neatly as I could, trying to keep the stacking pattern the Dragon was working on.

"I'll line them up, sir. I really appreciate your help, as I'm sure they all do."

"Thanks." I dusted the soot off of my hands using my embroidered, silk pants. Hard work wasn't beneath Ochana's crown prince, and I wanted them to know it. In the aftermath of the Galian riots, it couldn't hurt to remind everyone that I had the realm's best interests at heart.

I turned to get more boards but paused. Over my shoulder, I asked, "What's 'the Sanctuary'? I overheard the rip-out team mention it."

The Dragon instantly became a statue. His hand shook a bit as he replied, "I don't really know if... I mean, it's..."

Another Sien who I hadn't seen come out said from behind me, "Stop. Say nothing."

I looked between them, confused. "I'm sorry, did I say something wrong?"

He looked right back at me. "Prince Colton, we thank you so much for your help, and I'll be sure to tell everyone I can about the selfless thing you did here, but we're fine. We don't need any more help now, thank you."

He tossed his boards onto the pile, then turned around to go back without so much as another glance at me. The Dragon organizing the debris suddenly found his job far too interesting to talk to me anymore.

I took a deep breath. Well, I had tried to help.

With nothing else to do, I headed to the castle for the night. I'd probably get yelled at for all the black stuff on my silk slacks, but I kept playing in my head the weird way the Sien workers reacted to my merely mentioning Sanctuary, whatever that was.

I was so distracted with those thoughts, in fact, that I almost missed the small paper slip attached to my bedroom door. I pulled it off gently and flipped it over. It was a message, written in an oddly angular script.

I locked onto the "From:" field. Eva! I forgot all about Sanctuary as I read the message. It simply read:

• • •

Hi, Cole! Cairo and I r taking tomorrow off 2 come c u 4 a few days. I alrdy checked ur DragonTools calendar; don't u dare try 2 tell me ur bi-z, lol. Be there after brkfst!

I couldn't stop grinning at both her ridiculous spelling and the news. I unlocked the magic binding my door shut and went inside, but I went right to bed so I could be rested up when my two best friends in the world came to visit at last. I was so excited, though, that I couldn't fall asleep for hours.

CHAPTER 6

I almost slept through my alarm and kept hitting the snooze button. By the time I awoke enough to have a coherent thought, the one I had was to remember the news from last night.

No longer tired, I jumped out of bed, scrambled to my wardrobe, and reached for my dress-up clothes, but remembered at the last moment that they were covered in soot and ashes. I considered wearing my full formal outfit, but that thing was so uncomfortable.

I grabbed jeans and a green hoodie. To heck with it. My friends wouldn't care what I wore. I was in such a rush that I put the hoodie on backward and had to spin it around as I walked out my bedroom door.

After speed-walking to the kitchen, where I grabbed a couple bites of pancakes, I realized I was too high-strung to have much of an appetite, so I thanked the chef for lowering himself to making pancakes, then walked-jogged to the landing pads on Ochana's west edge. Naturally, I ended up sitting around and waiting, but mostly pacing back and forth as I was too excited to sit in one place for long.

After half an hour of waiting and two cups of coffee, though, even my enthusiasm faded a bit. I let out a huff and walked over to one of the park benches that lined the landing pads, where I plopped down.

The moment my rear end made contact with the bench, a red-and-gold streak raced up and arched over Ochana's ledge. My heart leaped from my chest just as I jumped from the bench and sprinted to the landing pad. I craned my neck trying to find them.

From above, Cairo and Eva, in their summoned Dragon forms, drifted down into view and settled like falling leaves on the pads. Both summoned their humans as they touched down.

I found myself taking the stairs to the elevated platforms two at a time and, grinning, ran to Eva and Cairo, wrapping one arm around each of them.

Cairo said, "Oof. Enough group-hug nonsense, Cole."

I could hear his grin in his voice though I couldn't see his face as I squeezed them tightly. I felt two warm embraces rather than just one.

"For Aprella's sake, act like a prince, you child."

Eva laughed. "Oh, shut up. You're just grumpy from flying."

"Possibly true," he replied as he and I took a step back from one another, "but right now, I could eat a cow. You don't happen to have a cow in your pocket, do you?"

Of course, street-food vendors were thick as trees in a forest around the landing pad district to offer tired fliers huge piles of raw meat or big platters laden with cooked food. He knew that as well as I, but his comment was a good reminder that my friends were probably exhausted. The Congo, where the Elven realm hid, wasn't exactly next door to Greenland.

I let go, grinning, and backed up a step. "Welcome home, Grumpy One and Grumpy Two. Let's go find a foodie so you can recharge your Mahier. It's my treat. How was the flight?"

Eva rubbed her shoulders with both hands. "Long. But it's good to be here. Hey, there's a good one." She pointed over my shoulder.

I followed her gesture and saw a mobile barbecue pit smoking merrily, its owners standing inside the kitchen they'd built into the wagon at one end.

As we drew near, a rich, mesquite odor hit me, and my mouth watered. "Looks good. Are you eating as humans or Dragons?"

"Humans," they both replied together, then looked at each other and laughed. Ugh.

The smells only got better as we got to the short line. When it was our turn, I ordered only a half-platter for myself, mostly to have something to look at while they ate, and five full-size platters. The merchant tried to give me the order for free, but instead, I slapped a Gold Crown on the counter, easily worth twice the food, and walked to the picnic tables with my friends and the receipts, thus denying the vendor any chance to keep trying to give his profits away.

Once their food was ready, we grabbed the huge trays laden with slow-roasted smoked beef haunch, cheeses, and high-potassium fruits. I tried not to watch them gorge on food, just nibbling my own. Only Dragons would have understood how they ate so much so quickly, but recharging was vital after any long flight, and especially after transforming a couple of times, as they had en route.

Sated, Eva leaned back on the bench while Cairo scarfed the last meaty morsels on his tray, and she patted her stomach. "So, Cole. Are you as excited to meet the new Dragons as I am?"

I glanced over. "What new Dragons?"

She rolled her eyes. "Oof. Don't tell me you're so busy you forgot about this year's New Dragons party. The celebration is tomorrow."

"Oh." My stomach sank. "So that's why you're visiting?"

The corner of her mouth turned upward, eyes sparkling with mirth. "No, stupid. I came to see my best friend and give the big idiot emotional support as he gives his first New Dragon speech."

I froze like a deer in headlights and groaned. "Speech?"

"Check your DragonTools app. Aprella only knows how

you missed an annual event, even without me around to keep your head out of the clouds."

I fished out my phone and tapped the button centered in the hard outer case's front cover. Opening like butterfly wings, the cover's two halves spun aside, pivoting on the bottom corners and rotating until they again came together under the screen to form the button pad.

I tapped the rainbow-colored dragon icon, and my tools suite filled the screen. At the top, marked Urgent, was a to-do notice: "Give speech at New Dragon party," and the date was tomorrow's. Ouch... "I guess I've just gotten used to my father sending servants to tell me what I need to do. I hadn't checked it in a while."

Eva smiled, rolling her eyes. "I figured. You'll see I attached a file to the reminder. That's a speech I wrote for you just in case you forgot and had nothing prepared. If you have something in mind, just ignore it."

"Thanks." I winked at her. "You know I don't have anything in mind. I'll use the one you so kindly wrote for me. But you already knew I would."

Cairo slid his now-empty tray farther down the bench and wiped his mouth with his forearm. "You know, I never understood why Ochana uses technology for these things. In Paraiso, they use their Tillium to set reminders."

Eva sat up straighter and put both her hands on my knee. "Oh, you should see what they do with it. Things we've never even thought of, as if we can only use Mahier to win a battle or something."

Cairo grinned at her. "She's enthusiastic. Did you know, she thinks our two kinds of magic were once related? I may agree with her."

"What do you mean?" I wondered if she forgot I could wield Tillium, but she seemed so excited that I asked the question I thought she wanted to answer.

"I can't use their magic, but I can sort of feel it when they wield it nearby. Both kinds feel sort of warm. I don't know, like a winter blanket. But you remember Mereum, right? Mer-magic feels cold and wet, kind of like the Merfolk themselves. Anyway, the Elves do a lot with Tillium that we do with our magic, but even more that we never thought of."

Cairo barked laughter, and under her withering glare, he shrugged. "Hah. My *Vera Salit* has already forgotten you use all three of those, and more. Plus, there's the whole 'we' thing."

"The '*we* thing'?" I paused, thinking back on what she'd said, and it hit me. "Oh, right. Because she's a Dramon, not a Dragon. I sometimes forget that, since she can use Mahier like us."

She glared at us both. "I forget nothing. And I know Cole can use it, but he's too stupid to think about how our magic *feels*."

It was my turn to laugh. "She has a point. I am stupid."

Cairo leaned back against the bench and interlaced his fingers behind his head. "I'll let you know when you say something that isn't true. But seriously, if you stop and pay attention, she's right. Mahier and Tillium feel almost the same. If they came from the same place, that could explain why you're so good with those two—and so bad with the mermaids' magic."

"I never noticed how they feel," I replied truthfully. I hadn't ever thought about it, though, so that wasn't a surprise.

Eva stood and began pacing in front of our bench. "Yeah, well, I have. Maybe just because I'm the only Dramon who can use our kind of magic, so I pay attention. But it's more than just feeling the same."

"I'll bite, again. How is it more?"

Still pacing, she said without looking at me, "I've been learning the Elven tongue, too. It's such a beautiful language, how it rolls off the tongue, and I think it's way better than English for making poetry. But when you know enough Elven, you start to notice how different Tillium incantations *feel*."

Cairo kicked my foot with his boot toe. "Get this, she says their spells feel like emotions. Like fire magic is angry, and healing makes her brain feel damp. That kind of thing. She's a lot better with their language than I am, though, so I just take her word for it."

The conversation continued, with Eva growing ever more excited as she talked about Paraiso, and especially about how egalitarian they all were down there in their Congo realm. It made me happy to see her so energized until the thought struck me that I might lose her to Paraiso. I felt bad about wanting her in Ochana, but it was the truth.

The more she talked, the more I realized something. Eva was figuring out what she wanted to do with her life, exploring her passions, living life—while I stayed there in Ochana, wasting my life on being a glorified guard. And for what? At least in the Time of Fear, I hadn't been just protecting Ochana's way of life, but saving all life on the planet. Now, I only protected Ochana, and...

I hesitated to even think the rest of that sentence. But it didn't matter, as the more I tried not to think it, the more I knew it was true: I didn't like the way Dragon society worked. It was a terrible setup for everyone but those at the top, the Leslos.

And I had to make a speech the next day to celebrate a bunch of new Dragons joining our society and abandoning the world they'd grown up in.

I got us moving as quickly as I could, after that. The more I had to listen to my best friend talk about how happy she was in Paraiso, away from me, the more I felt certain that she was the lucky one, not me, the crown prince. Plus, she had a soulmate to share it with, her *Vera Salit*. Only one of us was happy.

That was something, at least.

My formal uniform was about the least comfortable clothing I owned, but the king made me quit fussing with it. The outfit looked a lot like a tuxedo with a jacket that only brushed the top of the cummerbund-like accessory, but instead of being black, our "tuxiform" was a green shade so dark it looked almost black. The cut was reminiscent of a military uniform, but the piping down the trouser legs was emerald green, as it was for the jacket. What would have been a cummerbund on a human tuxedo here included a diagonal strip across the chest and over the left shoulder, like an ammo sash with decorative, non-functional pockets. Both were emerald green. The jacket and trousers had gold thread sewn in, forming a repeating pattern of stylized Dragon heads. The whole ensemble was made of thick silk, and I was glad the air conditioning kept the room at a comfortably cool temperature, so they didn't cling like saran wrap.

We held the party in the amphitheater with the dome closed to keep the outside heat outside. An orchestra played live music, but softly, the volume unchanging no matter where one stood in the big chamber. Whether that was done with magic or technology, I couldn't tell.

King Rylan and I stood behind a curtain, getting ready to enter the main area, and a sound dampener kept everything outside nearly silent save for the muted music.

"You ready for this, son?" My father smiled, adjusting my bow tie for the fifth time though I hadn't touched it since he'd last fiddled with it.

"Yes, I think so. By the way, where's Mom?"

"Neither of us like these things. Do you?"

I shook my head. "Not particularly, though I'm excited to see all the new Dragons."

"Right. So, we take turns hosting. This year, it's my turn. Have you a speech ready for later? I meant to ask you a few days ago, but my schedule kept me so busy..."

Again, I nodded.

"Good. Here, put in this earbud. Any time you look at someone's face, it'll whisper their name and title to you so you can greet them properly. I don't expect you to know everyone, much less the best title, but they will expect you to."

I sighed and put it in my ear. When I looked at him, a high-pitched woman's voice said, "His Majesty, King Rylan, ruler of the Dragon Realm and Lord of Ochana."

I said, "Your title is a mouthful."

He grinned. "That's just the *best* title for a formal affair. It's short and sweet. The full title takes even longer, I assure you. All right, let's get out there. We'll be spending a lot of time with Umbran and Trey Sepens, so—"

"Must we?" I tried not to frown.

"Yes, we must. Have you forgotten your manners so soon? They're family, and high-ranking ones at that. We haven't seen them in years, and it's appropriate to let them be seen among our close associates while they're here. It's also good politics."

Well, that was disappointing, but it was about what I expected. "Okay, behave like a prince. I get it. Ready when you are." Being a prince sounded far more exciting than it had turned out to be in practice.

We went through the curtain and made our way around

the room to greet mostly other important people. The unimportant people—the new Dragons who were the whole reason for the party—clustered in small groups, mostly ignored by these oh-so-important people. Once in a while, a dignitary would deign to stop and talk to a cluster of new Dragons for a few seconds before returing to their own kind.

My father and I were no different.

I spotted Trey from halfway across the room, but only once we drew nearer did he and his father, Umbran, make any effort to come to us. This despite the fact that we'd been announced as we came through the curtain. It seemed they wanted to bask in my father's reflected glory but wanted to pretend they were too important to go out of their way to do so. The thought irritated me.

Rylan, however, looked genuinely pleased to see them. "Duke Umbran, how are you and your son finding your stay in Ochana?"

Umbran's eyes narrowed while his son bowed slightly. "We are doing well enough, King Rylan. Thank you for your gracious invitation to the event. So far, our stay has been illuminating. Trey, why don't you and Prince Colton go mingle? The party is for new Dragons, after all, and I have something to discuss with our king." He looked over my shoulder and added, "I believe the Keeper of Dragons has friends arriving, as well."

Rylan nodded, giving me permission to run off. I turned to where Umbran had looked, and saw Cairo and Eva arriving, sans announcement. I frowned and headed toward them, uncomfortably aware of Trey's company.

Trey said, "I don't know what to make of you, Cole. You associate with Wolands, which is all well and good, but if I'm not mistaken, your other friend is a Dramon. I didn't know Dramon were so well connected these days."

"She's the Keeper of Dragons, too, Trey." I used his name without title, since he'd done the same, and felt a pang of pleasure at the irritation that flashed across his face. We were too close to my friends for him to say anything in return, though.

Eva and Cairo spotted me and waved as they came over. "Nice party, Cole," Eva said. "Who's your friend?"

My earbud whispered to me, though I wasn't looking at his face, "Count Trey Sepens, heir to Duke Umbran Sepens of the Duchy of Sepens."

I ignored the earbud. "This is Count Trey Sepens. His father is Umbran, a duke and a relative and friend of King Rylan's. Trey, this is Eva, Keeper of Dragons, and Cairo the Woland, her *Vera Salit*."

Trey smiled. "I was unaware anyone still believed in the myth of soulmates, but I am always pleased to meet those who honor the old traditions."

I shot a warning glare at Cairo, who looked away with his lips pursed, but Eva grinned. "Some myths have a kernel of truth, particularly among the Races of Truth."

"Indeed." Trey's smile faded a bit and he crossed his arms. "So, tell me, as a Dramon, what do you think of this

New Dragon celebration? I doubt you've seen one, of course."

"Excuse me?" Cairo cocked his head, eyes narrowing in a way that eerily reminded me of Umbran's.

Eva put her hand on his arm and gave him a wan smile, then looked Trey directly in the eyes with that wan smile frozen in place. "Count Sepens, what an interesting question. Yes, I've seen a New Dragon party before. This one isn't as big as that one was, but I like it fine, thank you."

"You have? I ask because you aren't a true Dragon. It's just surprising. There was a time when these Dragon parties were held to welcome, well... Dragons."

Eva's smile widened. "I understand your confusion. After Cole and I re-forged Ochana's alliances, creating the new Crowns Accord, then defeated the dark Elf King Eldrick when he invaded Ochana and everywhere else, the fine people of Ochana seemed to forgive my lack of proper pedigree."

I would have given much to be able to read Trey's thoughts as she gave her cheery rebuke with a smile. I half expected him to say something even more impolite, or storm away with his eyes narrowed like his dad.

Instead, he just nodded. "That, too, is interesting. Thank you for your service to Ochana, Keeper. The current king's father neglected his duties. Ochana suffered for it, as did the world."

"Thank you, I—"

"Perhaps if he'd kept our traditions, Ochana would have

led the other races of Truth in thwarting Eldrick early, rather than begging them for help later."

I fought my impulses and said evenly, "Times have changed."

"One need only look around this party to see that," Trey said. To Eva, he added, "Your opinion on this event's worth was really what I was asking."

"What's wrong with the party?" I had to stop myself from leaning forward, keeping my posture relaxed and my hands unclenched with an effort of will.

Trey's smile broadened, and he briefly uncrossed his arms to motion around the party. "It's a fine party, of course. I expect no less of any king. But look at all those noble Wolands."

Cairo looked around the room. "I don't know how many of them are noble, but what about us?"

"There was a time when it would have been quite a privilege for Siens and Galians to clink glasses with Wolands, much less with Leslos. You know what they say, 'the king sets the example.' The last king disregarded our traditions, so I guess it is little wonder that his subjects now feel entitled to rub elbows with Wolands."

Cairo shook his head slowly. "You may have noticed that the old king is gone. The king has changed with the times."

Trey shrugged. "So they have. Change is the only certainty when one can't rely on tradition to show us all the proper way of things. Rylan's father saw to that, and now we have castes mingling like equals. But we'll see what changes come next, when the new council meets."

I felt a tingle along the back of my scalp as he flashed a smile that was no smile at all.

Looking around the amphitheater at all the little clusters of people celebrating, I felt something off, something foreboding, though I couldn't put my finger on what was wrong. I decided it was just the present company.

CHAPTER 7

As the celebration continued, I kept getting sodas, avoiding champagne or wine. I still had a speech coming up, and if I gave myself any excuse to mess it up, I'd definitely do that. Eva, Cairo, and I made our way around the amphitheater to congratulate little groups of new Dragons and their families as we came across them.

Unfortunately, Trey diligently followed his father's instructions, and wherever I went, there he was, walking around with me. He either ignored whatever polite hints I gave or was too narcissistic to notice. That was entirely possible, I decided, based on the limited time I'd spent with him so far.

Every time he got out of earshot, Eva muttered under her breath, often clenching her fists in front of her and taking deep breaths. She was clearly just as fond of Trey as I was. Cairo, too, said little around the Sepens son, but I noticed he kept himself between Eva and him. Thank Aprella, they both had the good sense not to start a scene with Trey. Honestly, they had more restraint than I. I was hanging onto my civility by only a thread.

The other thing I noticed, besides Trey always at my side and the glances his father kept shooting us as he walked around with my father, was that the celebration's mood had shifted. The buzz of happy chatter had become muted, or so it seemed to me, though I was sure that perception had at least as much to do with my soured mood than any real change in the room.

At a quarter to nine o'clock, my ear bud whispered, "Colton, prepare for your speech. Fifteen minutes." It repeated the message at the ten-minute mark.

"Eva, Cairo, I've got to go get ready for my speech. I wish you could stand up there with me. My knees are knocking at the thought of speaking, but I have to do this alone." I shot a glance at Trey as I added, "It's a tradition."

"By all means, Prince Colton," Trey replied and inclined his head, "don't let us keep you from destiny and duty."

Eva, bless her, managed to keep from rolling her eyes. "Break a leg up there."

Cairo raised his eyebrow at that. "Don't break anything, in fact. Stay safe, Keeper. We'll see you when you're done embarrassing yourself."

"You're the embarrassment." I grinned at him, though my

stomach was already aflutter, and then gave Eva a hug before making my way toward the podium.

I was only halfway across the amphitheater when a spotlight glued itself to me. The background music faded to a whisper as King Rylan approached the podium. He cleared his throat, and magically, it sounded as though he were right next to me.

"If you'll pardon a proud father, here comes my son and heir, Prince Colton of Ochana, better known, perhaps, as the *Keeper of Dragons*. He has a few words he'd like to share with us all. Please give him a warm welcome, won't you?"

Every eye was on me as the conversations faded to silence. The only sound was my own heartbeat, racing in my ears. I had to remind myself not to wipe sweaty palms on my formal attire, and to smile and wave.

It was rough, making my way to the podium, and every step felt heavier than the last. Rylan stepped aside, backing out of the accursed spotlight that stayed on me every step of the way, leaving me alone at the podium with all eyes on me. In the back of my mind, I wished my mom were there to focus on while I spoke. My real mom, the woman who raised me, not the queen. As wonderful as my biological mother was—kind, cunning, intelligent, and I had grown to love her—I had one *real* mom, and I wanted her. But she was in Texas and would stay there.

"Ahem..." I cleared my throat, momentarily forgetting my opening line. I looked around the audience, buying time to remember my speech and gather my courage. I hadn't been this nervous when a giant Carnite had scooped me up, leaving only my head and feet protruding from its enveloping fist. And that was *really* nervous.

Well, I could fake it...

"Welcome to Ochana, your new home for as long as you want it, new Dragons."

I waved, making my waning smile wider, and tried to follow my father's advice of trying to make everyone present feel like I'd looked directly at *them* at least once.

The Dragons and their families applauded politely. Golf-clap, I thought, and abruptly, my fear was gone. That Carnite had wanted to eat me like a snack, and these people had nothing more dangerous than half-hearted applause. This couldn't hurt me. Fear was pointless. My plastic smile turned warm as relief flooded me. I could do this. My speech came flooding back to me.

"Every year," I continued, "we Dragons gather to welcome those who are just now coming home, rediscovering their true roots. Not so long ago, I stood where you do now. Only then, we were unaware of a shadow creeping up on us, the darkness of war. We had to reforge tattered alliances to have any hope of prevailing—regaining the trust of the Elves, the Trolls, the Mermaids, even the Fairies. But we prevailed. We witnessed the deaths of far too many of the world's Trolls—you may remember the pestilence that spread across the Earth. Yet, working together, Trolls and Dragons both still endure."

I let my smile fade and put both hands on the podium's edges.

"You, too, will prevail. You'll learn to breathe fire and to summon your Dragon at will. You'll learn how working together, each doing our share, we can not only win a war, but we can change the world for the better. We can overcome the shadows, just as you will overcome your fears of the new and unknown world you now find yourselves a part of."

I paused and leaned forward over the podium a bit as though to impress upon them the gravity of my words. "Working together, we can make this world better, you and I —not by relying on our king to do it for us, though we all know King Rylan never ceases to work toward that goal— but through a hundred little gestures, steps we can take each and every day. Your hard work, whatever your calling, is *your* gesture toward a better world."

I nodded, then put on an amused expression I'd practiced in the mirror. "Duty and loyalty, too, are powerful gestures. You are all Dragons, though, and you don't need me to tell you about honor. We each have a different calling, of course. To the Wolands is given unrivaled martial prowess. Like that word? I do. Prowess... It sounds amazing. But the Wolands aren't the only ones with prowess. Every time a Galian heals a wounded Woland, they show their prowess. Each time a Sien delivers supplies to our Guardian wings, striving in faraway aeries, bent on keeping the world safe from the next Eldrick, that, too, is prowess.

When a Leslo leads those wings in a charge against our enemy, placing themselves first in danger, that's *their* prowess."

I felt mighty impressed with myself. I'd messed up a bit, but I remembered the gist of my speech. I'd have to apologize to Eva later for messing it up. That thought brought a genuine smile to my face as I looked around at all the new Dragons.

I froze. Everywhere I looked, Dragons of every kind stood among only others of their own kind. Not only the older Dragons clustered with their own kind, but the new ones, too. What on Earth? These Dragons had come here as families, so they should have sorted themselves by family, not by color.

It felt all wrong.

I shook my head to clear the thought. "You new Dragons are no strangers to us. You're our children, our brothers and sisters, cousins, uncles and aunts... You're our family, whatever color your scales may be. Tomorrow, some of you will begin your training as Dragons. Some of you have trained almost a year now, and tomorrow will be just another training day. But for you both, new and less new, *you* are *my* family tonight."

I drew myself to my full, unimpressive height. "I welcome you to your new home. Welcome to Ochana. Enjoy the food and drinks, courtesy of King Rylan and the Sepens family. Dance. Meet new people. You'll have centuries to get to know them better, but there's one thing you can count on.

They're Dragons, *just like you*. Working together, you and I *will* change the world for the better."

I waved again, trying to look every person in the eyes—not that I could, with so many—and said, "Okay, enough terrible first-time speakers, right? Enjoy yourselves. Now, let's dance."

I strode from the podium with far more confidence than I felt, and as they applauded with far more warmth than they had when I first stepped up to the podium, I couldn't help grinning. What a rush that had been!

But in the back of my mind, I took note each time I saw Dragons standing only with their own color. Well, Trey was right about one thing—the world would keep right on changing. I vowed to make my speech a reality. We would change it for the better.

Twenty minutes later, I stood with Eva and Cairo, joking around now that Trey had finally left us alone for whatever reason. I didn't really care why.

Unexpectedly, King Rylan stepped up to the podium and tapped the microphone, and the orchestral music faded into the background again. "May I please have your attention?"

Cairo said, "Another speech, Cole? Why didn't you warn us?"

I shook my head, shrugging. "It's news to me. I hope everything is okay."

Rylan continued, "Ladies and gentlemen, and new Dragons of every kind, I hope you're enjoying your celebration. It's all for you, our progeny. And speaking of progeny, Duke Umbran Sepens has just advised me that his son, Count Trey Sepens, would like to speak to us all for just a minute. Where are you, Trey? Come on up."

He scanned the audience, and his gaze met mine. "Prince Colton, there you are. You too, come on up. This involves you, as well."

Cairo said in a half-whisper, "You know I hate your guts, Cole, but if you get the chance to duel him to the death, I hope you cheat like mad. What's this about?"

"Still no idea," I said. After a moment's hesitation, I made my way through the crowd and up onto the stage, joining Rylan at the podium.

Trey arrived a moment later, along with a Sien carrying a tray laden with champagne flutes. At the podium, he took one from the tray, then grabbed another and handed it to me.

With the spotlight on me, I couldn't just refuse, so I took it and nodded my thanks. I didn't have to drink it, after all. Champagne was definitely not a drink I enjoyed, having never had it before coming to Ochana. I assumed it was one of those things that's an acquired taste, as my father would have put it. It didn't hurt to be polite, though, especially with my father watching us.

Trey's voice rang out, deep and pleasant, carrying to every corner of the amphitheater through the magical microphone system, but it probably would have done so even without that. I imagined him practicing getting his voice to broadcast by shouting insults at his household staff across the manor.

"The Sepens family thanks King Rylan for his hospitality and for generously humoring a young Dragon with more enthusiasm than sense. Thanks for letting me speak, Your Highness."

Rylan nodded and held his hand out toward the crowd, inviting him to go on.

I spotted a familiar face in the audience, then. One I hadn't seen yet, though I'd been keeping half an eye out the entire time. In front, just outside the circle of light from the spotlights on us at the podium stood Arden, Umbran's daughter—through no fault of her own. She moved her hand to her mouth, head tilted slightly back, as though drinking. Then, she shook her head and pantomimed throwing a drink over her shoulder. I cocked my head, confused.

Trey's voice distracted me as he continued, "The Sepens have an age-old tradition I'd like to share with you all. And believe me, fellow Dragons, 'age-old' to a Dragon is a long time."

He paused a second for polite chuckles. "When a Sepens heir first meets the heir to the throne, the king has always allowed us the privilege of offering the heir apparent a toast. It's an honor and a privilege for me to continue that fine tradition now, in front of all of you fine people. May I, Your Majesty?"

Rylan smiled and repeated his earlier gesture. "Of course, Count Sepens. Our traditions bind us together."

Trey locked eyes with me, and grinned. "My father says that, too. Our traditions bind us together... Prince Colton, mighty Keeper of Dragons, you gave us all an honorable peace after delivering an unlikely victory in war."

He paused, and after a second, I said, "I... Yes, thank you. I didn't do it alone, though."

"No victory is ever won alone, Cole. We all fought, all over the world," he said, claiming some of our honor for himself, though I couldn't imagine him standing on the front lines with sword in hand. "We now gather from all over that same world to witness a new generation of Dragons coming home. Homecomings are a heady thing, aren't they? We're here to honor them, not ourselves, after all, so in return for delivering that victory, won't you please let me bind my family to yours by toasting our new Dragon family together? A toast, from us to them."

However much I disliked Trey before, I disliked him more now. Champagne was too fizzy, the flavor wasn't great, and the sharp aftertaste... Ugh. For a moment, I thought of tossing it, but with everyone watching us, it'd be an insult to turn down a goodwill toast. Whatever issue Arden had with drinking wouldn't make it any less of an insult, and I could practically hear my father's disapproving lecture later if I declined it.

Oh well. It wasn't the worst thing I had endured, or would, as the Prince of Ochana. "I'd be honored to share with the Sepens family a toast for Ochana's newest Dragons."

I raised my glass in return and drank, though I didn't toss back the whole glass as he had. The fizz burned my nose, the taste made me want to shudder, and I just couldn't make myself drink the rest. Instead, I just held the glass with my hand around the remaining liquid. After he came back down from the podium—ignoring me, thankfully—I made my way toward my friends and gave the half-empty champagne flute to the first server I ran across.

I had a duty to wander and mingle, greeting people and generally being seen doing it. The first people I greeted were a Woland officer and his Leslo wife, talking to another couple who were both in military dress uniforms like his. I didn't see their Galian son, who was among the new Dragons. The earbud told me all of that, of course—I didn't know any of them personally.

"Prince Colton, a fine speech, son. This is one tradition I'm glad the last king kept to," he said.

"Thank you. I agree, it's a nice way to welcome our newest members. So, has your son chosen a path, yet? Will he stay in Ochana?"

His wife laughed gaily. "Of course. This is our home, and

his. He knows his duty. He'll be a good ally and resource for our daughter when she takes over the family, someday."

The earbud whispered their daughter's name, a green Dragon. I'd have thought they'd split their estate, but that was family business and none of mine. "Of course. Where is he, by the way? I'd love to greet him personally."

He replied, "Oh, he's over there, somewhere." He motioned toward the amphitheater's horseshoe of stepped seating. "With the other blue Dragons, I imagine. So tell us, has King Rylan made any mention of bringing back the ranking lotteries among the blues and silvers? The old ways had much to recommend them."

I felt clammy. The ranking lotteries were just something in our history by the time I'd come to Ochana. They let the Fates dictate one's starting rank—heavily skewed by the family's social standing, of course. I almost told him my feelings about that, but instead, I shrugged.

"I don't know his plans. He has many important issues to deal with at the moment. But I'm sure that the idea will receive the attention it is due."

I made my excuses and continued on. I angled toward the stepped seating, but of course, I had to stop and greet everyone I encountered as I crossed the central space. Everyone I met was either a Woland or Leslo, it seemed, and they mostly seemed interested in a "Restoration," bringing back all those outdated old ways. The same old ways that had led to our alliances being in tatters when Eldrick made his bid to conquer the world, in fact. I smiled politely, said the king would consider their ideas, and moved on. The encounter repeated itself a dozen times before I reached my goal.

As only the central space had been well lit, it took a moment for my eyes to adjust to the dimmer sidelines. I hoped my concerns were unfounded, but as I moved deeper into the darker area, I saw a lot of new Dragons and families —all blue and silver. I greeted a few, but most didn't meet my gaze.

The parents present were likewise Galians and Siens, though many stood without their new Dragon children—if those were also blue or silver. The parents' responses to me were brief and rigidly polite. The kids, well, new adults… They just looked tense.

Alarm bells rang in my head. Something was going on, something I wasn't aware of. Maybe my father could tell me. I made my way back toward the central area to find him.

Before I got there, I heard a commotion to one side, along the wall. I squinted to see what was going on and saw it centered around one of the side doors. I didn't know what was happening, but something about it set my heart to beating faster, my adrenaline beginning to kick in.

Trusting my gut, I moved quickly toward the noise, keeping to the shadowy sidelines, and hoped my instincts were wrong.

CHAPTER 8

My clammy feeling grew worse as I approached the commotion, but when I drew near, all I saw were some Galians and Siens gathered around one of the drink-serving staff as she climbed to her feet. There was a serving tray on the floor amid scattered, broken glasses.

"What's going on, here?" I reached down to help the rising blue Dragon.

She didn't take my hand, and once on her feet, stood with hands together before her with her head down. The others were looking down, as well. She said, "My apologies, Prince Colton. A Woland knocked me down. He saw me coming through the door but didn't even slow down."

A Sien said, "I saw it, as well, Prince. He didn't even look back to see if she was okay, so we came to help."

Several were picking up the tray and bigger shards of glass, including a couple who were clearly not staff, but new Dragons, also blue and silver.

The room grew hotter still, and for half a second, I felt a wave of vertigo, but it passed. "Where is this Woland?" I didn't bother to hide my irritation. "I'll deal with it."

Everyone looked down, so I turned to look. The room seemed to keep spinning for a moment after I stopped turning, but I saw no red Dragons around.

I shook my head, but that sent the room rocking, so I stopped. "I'm sorry, but if you can't identify who did this, there's little I can do."

The woman who'd been knocked over pursed her lips, then replied, "It is quite all right, Prince Colton. I'm sure the Keeper of Dragons has more important people to help than one clumsy Galian. We'll make sure this gets cleaned up before a Woland slips or a Leslo steps on glass."

No one looked me in the eyes.

I couldn't help but frown. "I'm not sure what to say. Have I said or done anything to suggest I don't care about you because of the color of your scales? I really can't do anything unless you can point out the Dragon who did this. You're right, though—I have duties to see to, just like we all do. If you see the one who did this, let me know, okay?"

Mute silence.

I spun on my heels to go back to my vitally important job of shaking hands with people I didn't know, but a wave of vertigo hit me again. Maybe it was just me, but the room sure seemed hot... I wiped my forehead, but then had to put my hands on my knees to take a deep breath and steady myself.

The vertigo passed, and the room stopped swooshing to one side, so I again made my way along the shadowy perimeter, greeting people, but really, I was looking for Arden. I hadn't yet welcomed her officially, and my father would certainly expect me to do so.

Abruptly, my vision sort of... smeared to the left. No, that was to the right, right? I grinned. Why was that funny? I wiped my forehead with my sleeve, and it came away wet with sweat.

I had to find Arden. Rylan—he wanted me to? I walked through the crowd, looking for her. Everywhere I looked, the outlines on things were fuzzy, like my thinking. It sure was hot in here. Then, not far away, I spotted her. I decided I'd do my duty to greet the Sepens' new arrival, then go lie down and—

The floor shifted, like someone yanked a rug out from under my feet. I careened into something, and I heard someone shouting in outrage, but I didn't dare turn my head away from my target, Arden, or the vertigo would get worse.

Why did I need to talk to her? I couldn't remember. Maybe she would know. She seemed smart. Eva would like Arden. Maybe that was it, I decided. I'd get there, and then I'd introduce Arden to Eva. Then, I'd go to sleep off the damnable champagne, possibly right there on the floor. It didn't look that hard, actually. It looked furry.

The furry floor rose up and hit me. It was harder than I'd thought. I wasn't sure how, but it had smacked me and now kept pressing against me. All the people gathering around to look at the strangely behaving floor were standing sideways on it.

Or was I sideways?

Dizziness hit me, stronger than ever before, and the room swooshed up, up into a growing darkness. Then, I saw no more.

CHAPTER 9

Through the blackness, I couldn't see who was shaking me, but I didn't really care. My head felt like it was splitting open, it hurt so badly. The fog of confusion parted enough for me to realize my eyes were closed, though.

I cracked one eye open and winced from the daylight coming in through the amphitheater's open roof.

Someone I didn't recognize knelt, his hand on my arm, smiling down at me.

"Wha... Where am I?" I sat up. The pain flared, and I clutched my head with both hands as it slowly receded. My tongue felt like it was made of lead and tasted worse. "Who are you? Tell me what happened."

The stranger's smile widened into a grin, and other people who had gathered around were smiling, too. He replied, "Welcome to Ochana, the Dragon city, of course. As to what happened, my guess is you drank too much at the new Dragon celebration. There was a lot of that going around, last night."

Another face appeared, hovering over me. "Come on, new guy. Let's get you up. It's time for breakfast."

He extended his hand, and I grabbed it. "Ugh. I'm not sure I can eat. I feel like a wreck."

"Believe me, you don't want to miss it." The first one stood, making room, and took my other hand. "Breakfast is body fuel, after all."

"I just want to sleep," I tried to protest. It wasn't like I had anywhere else to be until the afternoon, when I'd have to take my wing on patrol. I wondered how many of them felt as ragged as I did.

"No chance. We look out for each other, so you'll just have to thank us later. Come on, sleepy-head."

They hefted me to my feet, one bracing me, as I wobbled, until I regained my balance. That took a few seconds. Then, they marched me across the amphitheater and out a door. Across the expansive parking lot outside, I saw a series of food trucks, some independent and others in Ochana's official colors, around which gathered a mob of Galians standing in line or sitting at the many tables to eat.

I wanted to protest. I wasn't hungry, and I would have preferred to eat at the castle kitchens than from any street-food vendors Galians could afford, but the idea of resisting took too much energy to think about, much less to exert.

Besides, my father would approve of his prince having breakfast with a gaggle of Galians, especially after the New Dragon Celebration party.

Oof... That reminded me that I'd just been awoken after passing out on champagne at that very party, and this photo-op breakfast might buy me a little leeway when he got around to "talking" to me about that performance. I had to assume he knew and was mightily upset, else he wouldn't have let them leave me passed out on the floor.

I sighed and let them drag-push me to the crowd. A couple Galians saw us coming, took one look at me, and got up to welcome me into their spot. I didn't necessarily like it when people treated Prince Colton differently than everyone else, but as shaky as I felt, I thanked them and plopped down on the picnic table bench.

In less than a minute, one of my two new comrades returned with a tray laden with food—bacon eggs, toast, juice... A healthy enough meal, I supposed, though it probably wasn't nearly as good as the castles.

After a couple of bites, my stomach settled down, and I realized how hungry I actually was. While I ate, I managed to relax a bit, and even enjoy the Galians' table banter. They were cheery, earthy, and it was obvious they looked out for each other.

By the time I was halfway through, I felt a lot less shaky, as well. I smiled at my two rescuers. "Thanks for doing this. I'm feeling a lot better, now."

They smiled in return. One said, "You're welcome. And

welcome to Ochana. Just remember, we all take care of each other. Return the favor to someone else when you can, and you'll get along great here."

"Wait, what?" I cocked my head. Confused, I replayed what he'd said in my head. "Oh, you don't recognize me?"

He grinned. "Are you one of those 'famous for being famous' dragons, or did you do something interesting?"

The other one laughed. "We got a celebrity with us this morning."

I found myself grinning with them and feeling my cheeks grow warm. I'd just assumed they knew me the whole time, but really they were just being nice to a stranger with an ego too big for his own good, as it turned out.

"Ouch. I thought everyone knew the Keeper of Dragons just by looking at them. Boy, are my cheeks red—"

Riotous laughter all around the table cut me off, and one said, "Uh oh, better call the media, let 'em know the Keeper is back."

The other said, "Kid, the Keeper left last night. She's probably back gallivanting with the Elves again, by now. Newsflash, you don't look like her."

The first one nudged the other with his elbow. "Oh, get real. He's just kidding. There's only one Keeper, and he isn't it. Right?"

I looked down at my hands, my clothes. Everything looked fine to me... My hands, my green sash, my uncomfortable green uniform-tuxedo outfit... "I'm Cole, still. What do I look like to you guys?"

The first one, the one who'd woken me up, still grinned at me. "Wow. Well, I'm Perry. Pleased to meet you, Cole. What do you mean, 'what do you look like'? I guess you could have stolen the sash.

The second one laughed. "Who'd want to?"

Perry continued, "But you can't hide the blue eyes. You're a Galian, of course."

The other one rose and clasped my shoulder. "All right, enough joking around. It's almost time for the Assigning. Welcome to Ochana, brother."

I was so stunned that I almost missed that last part.

CHAPTER 10

"Okay, listen up." Perry stood before a group of new Galians. "I've met all of you individually, but this is the first time I'm addressing you together. Probably the last time, too, though I hope to see each of you around Ochana from time to time. Say hi if you see me. But that's not why we're gathered, is it?"

He paused, looking around the little crowd.

I did the same. I kind of felt bad for them. Last night, we'd all partied at a gala event, but today, there were no parties for Galians. Their faces made it clear they knew it, too.

Someone said, "So, tell us why we're here. Tell us what you want."

Another added, "What you really..."

"...really want," finished a third one.

Perry grinned. "Speaking of that, feel free to sing while you work. It makes the hours go by faster. Remember, your only friends are other Galians. Sometimes, you might find a friendly silver, but the Siens are the only ones you can trust as far as your human can throw a Dragon. Galians, though, all share your journey, even the ones you don't get along with, and we stick together. *Always* stick together. Without your brothers and sisters, you have nothing. So, among ourselves, have friends and enemies, but it has to always be us against the world. Never betray that, and you'll be fine... Tired, but fine."

Duly noted. I hoped I wouldn't look like one of them for long. The only reason I was going along with the farce was that I figured I could talk to some of the reds and greens I knew if I managed to get castle duties. Soon, with any luck, I'd trade my broom for a sword. For the moment, though, I paid attention to every word Perry said.

Someone else asked, "What kind of jobs will we get? My human parents did their best to get me ready for this, and they never hid the truth. They said we were 'nurturers,' whatever that means."

The other Galian who'd first helped me up stood beside Perry, though I hadn't yet heard his name. He said, "Good question. It means that many of us are healers, trained both in mundane medicine and to use Mahier for healing. You'd be surprised how often Dragons get injured, but Healer is a pretty easy job. If you aren't a medic, the rest is up to someone else. We'll go see her and get whoever is left all sorted. It could be anything from tending the nursery to working with the Sien farmers to 'magic' the heck out of the crops. There's lots of jobs we do. But like I said, that's someone else's decision. I'm just here to get you all oriented and help you figure out what you'll be doing."

"Can we make requests? Is she nice?"

Perry frowned and shook his head. "You can ask, but she puts us where we're needed."

The other Galian said, "No, she's not nice, but she is fair. No one here is 'nice,' kid. She looks out for Galians the best she can, which is what I'm doing, too."

Perry smiled and added, "She tries to take your preferences into account. She really does. But at the end of the day, she answers to someone, just as I do. Just as you'll soon do."

"Ochana looks like straight glamour on the outside," the other one said, motioning around to indicate all of Ochana, "but as you're about to find out, this whole place would stop working if we did."

Perry nodded. "It's true that we don't have the glory of the Wolands who protect us all, or the privilege of our Leslo leaders who make the big decisions, but there's honor in what we do. Hold your head high, cast your gaze down, and remember that the whole realm stands or falls on how well we do our jobs."

The other Galian said, "Okay, folks. I hope you all got enough to eat this morning, because free time is over. Follow

Perry, and we'll get each of you settled in and assigned a job."

He turned and motioned over his shoulder for us to follow, and after a moment's hesitation, I found myself doing what all the new Galians did—follow instructions, and follow Perry heading east.

We passed the amphitheater, now closed of course. We passed the manors, too. Shortly, we entered a densely packed neighborhood where the landmarks looked familiar. A tree here, a lamppost there. I was pretty certain we went by the burned-out blocks from the riot, but brand-new buildings now stood where the husks had been. They looked like nice apartment buildings, though, where houses had stood before.

Ahead, a big park loomed. We walked by a hospital, where gowned Galians moved to and fro, but most of the people I saw in the waiting room, through the big, paned-glass windows, were Siens. I wondered if those were the ones who got hurt "surprisingly often," as our guides had said, or if we were merely in a Sien neighborhood. If we were, I didn't see any people around to show me whose neighborhood it was, given that everyone was probably at work or asleep.

When we reached the park, we didn't turn left or right, as I'd expected, but kept right on walking through the broad gate and into the park itself. It was lush and green, but it bore no resemblance to the manicured gardens of a Leslo park. Instead, it was mostly just grass and trees with a little picnic area off to one side.

It was to that picnic area they herded us, and over the other Galians' heads, I saw a woman standing atop a picnic table, facing us with her hands clasped behind her back. Fifty or so of us Galians gathered around her, then Perry and the other one approached her and shook hands. She immediately put her hands behind her back again and nodded to them, smiling.

When she turned to face us, the smile was gone. "Okay, Galians. My name is Myrta, and I'm the one responsible for making sure the jobs get filled. I'm sure you're tired of hearing this, but welcome to Ochana. You already got the rah-rah speech, so I'll spare you another. First, medical. Any of you who have formal medical training, step over to Perry, over there, and stand by."

Everyone looked around at the others. A couple hesitantly raised their hands.

Myrta growled, "I didn't stutter. Let's go, people, get over by Perry. We don't have all day."

Almost a dozen Galians looked around nervously, then trickled over to one side, where Perry and the other had separated themselves.

The woman nodded, apparently satisfied. "Good. That's plenty. You might not be old enough to be full-fledged human doctors, but with some help from our Mahier instructor, you'll soon be masters at healing Dragons and humans alike. Those of you with *real* aptitude might catch a break and be sent to an Earth medical school for that extra special human touch. Mahier can run out, you know, and our instructors can't just wiggle their noses to teach you humans' magic-free medicine."

She turned to the rest of us, maybe three dozen nervous-looking Galians, and for the first time, smiled at anyone but the welcome duo. "To the rest of you, I apologize in advance if you don't end up with your dream job. Not everyone gets a cushy doctor's office. But don't worry too much—at least you aren't Siens."

She chuckled, then her smile faded and she was all business. "Next up. If you are great at a musical instrument—and I mean record-deal good, not weekends in the basement—then come here. One at a time, please."

Only three approached, which drew a frown from her. The frown deepened when the first one proudly proclaimed with a grin that he was a concert-level cellist.

"The orchestra is full, and no one's asking for cello lessons we can't cover already. Sorry, back with the rest, please. We'll get you something easy on your hands, though, until a spot does open up somewhere."

As the glum cellist came back to the rest of us, the other two, a guitarist and a bass player, were told there were Leslos needing lessons, and silver Dragons didn't stoop to being merely music teachers.

As we watched a Galian assistant herd the two musicians away, a thought occurred to me—Myrta would know who belonged in the castle, and would know the crown prince was missing. Surely by now, people like Myrta had been told to look for me. Even if I didn't look like me, she had the authority to send me to someone who could fix my little problem. I didn't really want everyone laughing at me again, though, so I inched my way to the back of the crowd and made sure everyone else got sorted before I did.

One by one, people went up to Myrta. She looked each person over carefully, and I sensed her using Mahier with each person. What was she doing with magic? Whatever it was, she ended each inspection with a satisfied nod and declared their future career with as much assurance as a DMV clerk issuing a driver's license.

Most of them ended up being staff and personal assistants for Woland officers and Leslos. A few lucked out and got to be artists of different types, though one, who'd been told he would make world-famous clay figures, nervously explained he had no artistic talent. Myrta told him he was wrong and sent him on his way.

The crowd slowly shrunk, and my turn approached until, finally, I was the only one left with Myrta, save for one last assistant hovering in the background to take me wherever she decided I'd have to spend the rest of my life. But I was the crown prince... I just had to make her understand the situation, and I'd be back in my own bed, wearing my own clothes.

"Interesting," she said, looking me up and down as she had the others.

"You know me?" Finally, someone who might be able to help resolve this mess!

"No," she replied, crushing that ember of hope. "Your Mahier feels off, somehow. Not like everyone else's. Any idea why that might be?"

I had one really good idea as to why, actually. "Yes. Listen, things aren't quite as they seem. You know the Keeper of Dragons, right?"

"Of course." Myrta frowned. "Everyone knows her. She's the Dragon who ended the Time of Fear. I don't know her personally, but who doesn't know of her?"

Gah, I wanted to scream. Instead, I took a deep breath and then said as evenly as I could manage, "Until yesterday, there were *two* who are the Keeper of Dragons. Eva, and King Rylan's son, Prince Colton. Until yesterday, I was—"

She interrupted me, barking, "Stop this foolishness. The king has no children, so you can hardly be a prince, and there's one Keeper, which is why it's not 'Keepers.' You tell me—what does that mean?"

I stared, open-mouthed. "What?"

She snarled at me. "It means you're not a prince, and you're not a second Keeper."

"No, you don't understand, I—"

"Stop, I said. Do you have medical experience?" She glared, leaning forward, though I didn't think she even realized she was doing it.

I was treading on thin ice, at risk of making an enemy I could ill afford to make. "No..."

"Fine." Her grimace turned into a smile, yet her jaw muscles stood out from clenching her teeth. "You cook a ridiculous story. Let's hope you do better with food. You're in the kitchens, pal." She turned to the man with her and shouted, "Kitchens. Get him out of here."

Stunned, I didn't even think to resist, and wouldn't have had the will to do so if I had.

"Hey, new kid." The cook spun on me, kitchen knife in hand. "We're almost out of potatoes. Get over to the warehouse and bring five more cases. It's two blocks—I'm sure you saw it on the way here."

I nodded.

"Well then, hurry, or you can be the one to explain to the Wolands why they have half a dinner."

He turned back around, ignoring me completely, just as he had for the other two hours I'd been working in the kitchen except when he was yelling at me.

I got out as quickly as I could. Instead of turning right, to head to the warehouse, I turned left. West, toward the landing pads. At the pads, I glanced at a tall tower clock nearby and paused long enough to think of where the patrol wings would be, given the standing schedule for the week—a schedule Prince Colton, Keeper of Dragons, Prince of Ochana, and leader of a wing, had helped devise.

Then, I walked a path skirting the edge of Ochana's floating disc.

As soon as I thought no one was looking, I stepped over the edge—and fell. I slowly counted to five before I summoned my Dragon and felt my spirits rise along with my scaly hide as I banked to the southeast and flapped hard to speed up. Faster and faster still. At the same time, I let myself begin to absorb Mereum from the water vapor in the clouds I flew through.

About the time I reached Africa's coast, my Mahier half gone, I switched to my accumulated Mermaid magic to maintain a bubble of still air around me, flying as fast as I possibly could. I stopped only long enough to devour a cow, ignoring the freaked-out bovines mooing all around me, and in only a few minutes, I was airborne again and stuffed with delicious, fresh meat, savoring the coppery taste of its blood as I departed.

By the time my Mer-magic ran out somewhere over the Sahara, I'd digested the cow and my Mahier was again full. By the time I spotted Paraiso's magic glamour disguise deep in the Congo, I still had plenty of Mahier remaining.

I angled my path to land just inside that camouflage shell, summoning my human as my feet touched the jungle floor, and jogged the rest of the way in. Keeping my leg muscles fueled with Mahier was easy compared to the drain of flying at those speeds, much less transforming, and I barely dented my remaining Mahier pool. I also started to absorb more Mereum, along with Tillium—the Elven magic was plentiful here, and I'd absorbed my fill of Tillium well before I'd half-refilled my Mereum.

As I entered Paraiso proper, I slowed to a brisk walk along the well-lit jungle floor. The city teemed with Elves and a few Trolls, but none gave me more than a curious look. To them, I must have been just some random Dragon—not their usual visitor, perhaps, but not the oddity it once was, thanks to *me,* dammit.

From the city's outskirts, I headed toward one massive tree in particular among the many that held the Elven city off the ground. Eva or Cairo must still be there somewhere, as they had only left Ochana again that morning.

I was still several trees away from my goal when two familiar people *popped* into existence in front of me. Eva and Cairo immediately began to walk my way, deep in a conversation that must have started before they blinked from treetop to ground, the only acceptable way for Paraiso's Elven residents to get down.

Whether they'd moved tree houses since I'd last been there or they'd been visiting among their Elf friends, I didn't know. They had to be leaving, though, or they'd have been up on the bridges that stretched like a spider web between the tree-buildings.

I moved into a shadow, and it was hard to catch my breath. I counted to ten as I followed them with my eyes, gathering my courage, and then followed. I guess I needed to count to ten again, because I was still shaky. Anyway, I needed to approach them when they weren't right next to any of the many Elves moving to and fro. If they recognized me, I didn't want anyone else to know. Someone had done this to me, and I had no idea who might let my presence slip to the wrong ears.

When they stopped beneath a light atop a tall post—a light with no flame, steady and strong like the Tillium that surely powered it—I breathed a sigh of relief when I realized no Elves were nearby.

I stepped from the shadow and walked toward them. Would they recognize me? I sure hoped so. Of all the people in this world, if anyone could see through whatever magic hid me, they could.

I told myself that over and over, willing my feet forward...

About twenty feet away, I entered the sphere of light from the lantern and didn't slow down. Both their heads came up, noticing me at almost the same moment.

I stopped and found myself smiling at them despite myself. They *had* to know me. Eva and Cairo couldn't possibly be fooled by a mere glamour. Could they? In the back of my head, I wondered how a mere glamour made everyone in Ochana forget the king had a son, but when seconds ticked by without them asking who I was, my grin grew.

"You do know me." A weight I'd hardly been aware of lifted from my shoulders.

Cairo rolled his eyes like he had done so often with me.

"Sure, pal. You're a new Dragon, obviously, and a Galian at that. Should I know you?"

Eva glanced at him, then back at me. "Are you a fan?"

I blinked a couple of times and heard myself saying, "I can't believe... You don't know me? This is really happening?"

Cairo's lip twitched, but Eva just looked bemused. "Oh, honey, if anyone knows how hard it is to be the new guy, it's me. But if you're having a hard time fitting in, just give it time. It's only been a little while. I promise, it gets easier."

She snapped her fingers, like she'd just come to some epiphany. "You know who you should talk to? A Galian named Jules on the Dragon Council. You could go in the morning, even, and say I sent you."

As her smile grew—like she'd done me some huge favor—I could only shake my head, disbelieving. This wasn't happening... I had to go. I had to get out. The jungle closed in on me, and I needed space, air beneath my wings. I turned and walked away, and they just let me.

I only paused once, looking back to say more harshly than I should have, "Jules isn't on the Council anymore."

Too much. All the effort to get there, all the months we'd spent together, they meant nothing.

A moment later, I flapped up, into the sky, determined never to go back to fetching potatoes for warriors who didn't even know me—and equally, knowing I had nowhere else to go. I couldn't even just go back to my old home, to the humans who had raised me. I'd certainly be a stranger to them if my two best friends in the world didn't know me.

For the first time in my life, I realized my Dragon form couldn't cry. Even tears were denied me.

I flew, angry and fast, closer to the speed of sound than I think I'd ever gone. My shoulders ached from the effort, and the ventral edges on my wings were wind-sore in spite of my shield—and the burn felt good. At least the aches and pains were *real*. That pain was no illusion, no lie like my entire life had become.

Near Africa's Mediterranean coast, I caught sight of a herd of goats down below and dove, mindless with hunger. I hadn't been conserving Mahier or drawing Mereum, and the Tillium magic I'd gathered in Paraiso was long gone. I only remembered to shield myself about fifty feet up, a split second before I collided talon-first with a goat. I was glad it didn't suffer, but I made no apologies to its fellow goats for devouring it in huge chunks, barely bothering to chew.

Still hungry, I leaped on another goat that stood nearby, immobile with Mahier pinning it in a sort of stasis—I'm not cruel—and I didn't allow it to suffer, either. I made sure of that. But I needed a lot of food right then and there. Nor did I allow myself to digest the meat in my gullet before leaping back into the air without bothering to clean up my mess.

My anger had abated a little, along with my hunger, and

the heavy meat slowed my flight. It was well past one o'clock when I landed in Ochana again, staggering as I hit the landing pad and shifted into my human, exhausted beyond tired.

But where could I sleep? My room in the castle wasn't my own, nor were my barracks with what had been my wing of Wolands. The park? No one would be there at this time of night.

I headed that way. In the morning, I'd have to endure whatever lecture Myrta deigned give the Prince of Ochana for not fetching potatoes, but that was tomorrow's worry.

I almost bumped into someone walking into my path from a side road and looked up—only to recognize Arden. The white Dragon. I looked down and kept going, my vision blurring as they welled up. Just one more person who wouldn't recognize me.

"Cole?"

I stopped mid-step and took a deep breath. No way, it was my imagination, it had to be. I turned around...

...Arden collided with me, wrapping her arms around me in a tight embrace. "Cole, it is you! Damn you, I was so worried. You passed out, and then I couldn't find you. Where on Earth have you been? Are you okay?"

Her words spilled out, but I hardly heard them. I just stared, and my welling eyes finally spilled over.

It was over. Someone... Someone knew me. Thank Aprella. But how was it possible?

CHAPTER 11

Arden cocked her head, raising one eyebrow as she pulled away from me, keeping her hands on my shoulders. "Are you... okay?"

I started to say I was fine. I started to say it was all okay. But why should I lie? And just like that, a dam burst inside me, and my anger and confusion and yes, my fear, all poured out of me in a torrent of words. I couldn't stop that torrent any more than I could stop the river of tears streaming down my cheeks no matter how many times I wiped my eyes.

Through it all, she stood still, listening, nodding. When I told her of Eva and Cairo, even her eyes got misty. When I was done unloading it all on Arden, she took a deep, ragged breath. For a moment, she pursed her lips and got a faraway look in her eyes, then the focus returned.

She nodded once, sharply. "Okay. I know where to take

you for the night, at least. You'll be safe there, and we can figure out what to do next. I have some things to tell you, too, but not here."

She led me back toward the landing pads but stopped at the bottom step. "Cole, can you fly? Do you have enough magic left to summon your Dragon? It's not far."

"Yes. I've got some left." I didn't need to tell her about all that Mereum in the air from the huge waterfall endlessly flowing over Ochana's edge, but I'd been drawing it in ever since I realized she actually recognized me.

"Good. We'll wait until no one is looking, then just drop. When we're about five hundred feet up from the snow. Dragon up, level out, and follow me."

When no one seemed to be looking our way, we stepped over the edge hand-in-hand. My stomach lurched as gravity took over.

Arden folded her arms back, and she shot away from me, streaking downward.

I copied her move, and caught up.

Grinning like an idiot, she flipped over, falling backward to face me, then extended her arms and legs. I shot past her, hearing her laughter in the wind as I raced by. I flipped over, too, and did the same move.

It was like flying. Humans, flying. We zigged and zagged, spun and flipped. Like dolphins playing on waves of air, we chased each other and laughed. It felt good to laugh again.

Of course, Greenland raced up to meet us, and at her

thumbs-up, we both summoned our Dragons. In the half-second before my mental shield went up through force of habit, I could still hear her laughter in my mind.

Spiraling, we circled far slower than before, my third phalanx, or "finger" tip, inches from hers. Our phalanges almost touched for another entire circle—yet another game of "how close could we stay," with one circling on the inside and the other on the outside arc.

Ha, that one was almost perfect, she beamed her thought directly to me. I had to agree, it was nearly a perfect tandem spiral, better than my wing had managed on training maneuvers in fact.

Below, nearly one hundred miles north of Narsaq, Greenland, the seemingly flat glacial center filled my view, but Arden banked a few degrees west and then straightened out. We came in low, then leveled out, skimming a hundred feet above the blank ice sheet.

It wasn't until almost the moment we landed that I saw a feature in that featureless ice. A low, rocky crag rose up only a couple hundred feet, dead ahead, and she flew straight for a spot about halfway up.

Slow as you can go, she thought-spoke to me, and then she did just that. I followed suit until I felt certain the air would fall out from under me—and then I saw it. A large hole in the side of the hill, a cave with a flat outcropping right outside. It wasn't nearly large enough for two dragons, but she summoned her human form at the outcropping, and landed lightly on her feet.

I staggered a bit as I landed, as I'd had to fly a little faster than her due to my heavier dragon-weight, but I narrowly avoided landing on my face. When I turned to face her, she was grinning broadly.

"I saw nothing," she said, voice light and airy.

I looked back at the cave. The entrance was perhaps ten feet high, about the same in width. "I'm pretty sure it'll take less Mahier to stay warm in there."

"I'm sure you're right. C'mon, it's safe. I've been here before." She headed to the opening.

Inside, it was apparent someone had cleared out the snow and ice, likely with dragonfire judging by the universally bare stone. Inside, the cave ceiling rose sharply to about twenty feet up, and it was about the same depth and width. The walls were smooth and joined the floor at a neat, 90-degree angle.

"What is this place? It's no natural cave. There are none, here." Along the back wall, I spotted a mound of dry wood, a couple of crates, and a wooden spool of the sort humans use to stretch cable, set like a little table. Some furs lay heaped up next to the ashes of a dead fire.

"No idea. I found it on one of my illicit outings before that first time you spotted me. Maybe a troll's cave once?"

"Ha. Hardly. Trolls live in the earth, but they don't live in caves, despite what you may have heard. Not like this, certainly. Does anyone else know of it?"

"Nope." She walked to the wood and began to set up a fire. I wondered if she'd yet mastered producing small flames in human form—Jericho had taught me the trick—but instead, she pulled out a lighter. "I kept it a secret. It's a decent place to digest a sheep before flying back, but mostly, I wanted a place of my own. My own room back at the manor in Ochana isn't exactly my sanctuary."

"Hm. I'm sorry to hear it. How are things at... home?" I wished I had something to say that would make it better for her.

"The best part for me is that my father and brother spend all their time out of the house. While they're gone, it's not so bad, though I'm still restricted to the manor grounds and forbidden to be a Dragon."

"You are a Dragon," I replied.

"You know what I mean. I can't summon it. I'm kind of afraid to find out what Father would do if I disobeyed that one. I doubt he'd hurt me, but I'm quite sure I'd be restricted to staying indoors. At least I can walk around outside, and the grounds are large enough so I can escape to myself when I need to."

"Where were you going when I bumped into you?"

A small ember caught and flamed in the small pile of wood amid stones. She looked up at me, and then stood, dusting off her hands.

"I was looking for you. I had no idea where you went after that so-called celebration. I can't tell you what a relief it was to see you walking around. I had worried that my father and brother..." She looked down as her voice faded out. Fidgeting with her fingers, she said, "Why did you walk right by me? You acted like you didn't recognize me, at first."

"More like I was worried you didn't recognize me. I passed out at the celebration, and when I awoke, no one knew me. They say there's only one Keeper of Dragons, and I'm not her. King Rylan has no children, they say… and I'm a Galian."

Her gaze lifted, eyes roaming over me. "You look like you, to me. Your Dragon looked like you, too, with all those pretty colors shimmering. But no one else?"

I shook my head.

"What about Eva and Cairo, your friends?"

"Nope. They saw a blue Dragon, too, and a new one at that. I have no idea why, but it's been… eye opening."

"Weird doesn't cover it." She pursed her lips, eyes shining icy-white light for a moment. "My family is planning something. I don't yet know what, though I'm trying to find out more. Clearly, it involved getting rid of you. It had to be that drink Trey handed you. I tried to warn you, you know."

Well, in hindsight, that was abundantly clear. It also explained the odd taste. "Some kind of potion, maybe. Did you eat or drink anything at the party?"

"No, we ate dinner right before coming to the New Dragon ceremony. Why?"

"Just a thought I had. I hadn't had anything to eat or drink at the event, either, though Trey kept trying to get me to the refreshments. I just kept telling him to go on, then, if he was thirsty. I was trying to get rid of him anyway, but he stayed glued to me the whole time."

She pursed her lips, nodding. "Then they forced your hand. So, something in the food, maybe. It's the only way it could affect everyone at once short of a spell of some kind, and I'd hope we would have felt that. But you passed out, where the others didn't, so maybe not."

It occurred to me that they might have had to add their potion to a drink at a moment's notice and misjudged how much to use. I doubted Umbran stood around for an hour with a warm drink in his hand, waiting for the chance to get me to take it. Why else would he have had Trey following me around, trying to get me to eat or drink at the buffet?

But that was all conjecture. I didn't know anything for certain, other than that it had ended horribly for me. "I don't know. Try to find out what they did, though. Maybe in knowing, we can figure out a counter for it. In the meantime, what should I do?"

Really, I just wanted to stay in that cave and hide, and hope this potion or whatever finally wore off. I doubted that hiding there would get my life back, though. "I need a plan."

"Yeah, *we* do need a plan," she said with a wan smile. "My father and brother leave the grounds every morning. If you need to get in touch with me, you can slip a note through the fence on the southwest corner before you go to work, and I'll try to come wherever you tell me in the note. If I can."

"Work?" I frowned at the thought. That did not sound like getting my life back.

"Of course, stupid. You have to behave, do your job, not make waves. We don't want any kind of commotion that could draw attention to you. What if my father or his agents are looking for you?"

I let out a long breath. That confirmed my suspicions—hiding in that cave was not an option. I'd have to throw myself on Myrta's mercy and hope she didn't make me go dig ditches or something, like a Sien.

Like a Sien... How unfair was that? They were Dragons, and their labors kept Ochana running, yet they got less respect than Galians. I hadn't really noticed that before. Now, looking back with a new perspective, the point was as sharp as a dagger.

"What are you thinking?" Arden put her hand on my shoulder lightly.

Grimly, I replied, "I'm thinking I see things differently than I once did, and hoping I someday get the chance to do something about it. In the meantime, I'll do just what you suggested. I'll go back, and whatever they tell me to do, I'll do it until we come up with something better."

For the next couple of hours, I tried very hard not to think about my own problems or Ochana's, and just enjoyed that little window of normality with someone who knew who I was and wasn't scheming against me. It was good to be Cole again, if only for a little while. That only made heading back that much more somber.

Though we didn't turn her cell phone back on until we were back in Ochana lest she be tracked, Arden had her normal access to DragonTools. It wasn't hard to find out what I needed to know, with her help.

Shortly after the sun arose, Myrta came into the park right on schedule, accompanied by a couple of assistants. I took a couple of deep breaths, steeling myself for the conversation, and then approached her. I stopped a little over ten feet away and waited for her to acknowledge me.

I had to wait a nerve-wracking five minutes before she finally looked at me. "For Aprella's sake, what is it, new one?" She looked as frustrated as she sounded.

"I'm so sorry, Myrta. You assigned me yesterday to the castle's kitchens, and—"

"And you ran away in the middle of your scheduled shift, leaving everyone else to carry your load. Outstanding job of letting everyone else do your job for you, by the way. How should I expect someone to behave who claimed to be King Rylan's son, though?"

"Wait, what do you mean by that?" My pulse sped, and it was a struggle to keep the smoke from coming out of my nose. He might not remember me, but that was my father she was talking about… in a way.

"I mean that no son of King Rylan would abandon their duties, much less leave their work for others to do. Our king does not leave others to do his job, nor would his son." She met my gaze and held it evenly.

"I… Actually, that's what I wanted to talk to you about. I

owe you and them an apology. I can only say that I was homesick and considered leaving. But now, I want to make it up to you both. I know my place now. I'm sorry."

She watched me intently, eyes narrowed, chewing the inside of her cheek. After a moment, she nodded. "Okay. That's a start. But let me ask you this—why did you not go back to your Earth home if you were so homesick?"

I lowered my gaze, focusing on her shoes. I'd learned that others thought it made me look contrite, and I had a lot of practice at it from my most insecure, early days on Ochana. "I thought that it might bring trouble onto them. They raised me, and though I haven't shown it, they raised me well. I couldn't do that to them, that's all."

Her expression softened, eyes relaxing around the corners. "At last, something worth hearing comes from your mouth. That's the reason—the only reason, mind you—that I'm willing to give you another chance at the kitchens in the castle, where you can find the help you need with whatever delusions make you think you're a prince. Either way, it's only right to give you a second chance. It can't have been easy to apologize for being lost on your first day and making a rash decision."

I lowered my head further, bowing. "Thank you, Myrta. When can I start?"

"You *may* start in an hour, relieving the night shift and breakfast crew. You will likely have to earn your forgiveness, if I know Rogan, but if he says he forgives you, you can believe it. He's hard, but as fair a person as I've ever known."

"Thank you. I can't—"

"Get out of here, newbie."

"Yes, ma'am." I scurried away, heading toward the castle. My castle. My home. Someday, it would be that again. For the first time, I felt certain that I could resolve this. I didn't have any reason to think so, but my gut told me so. I was beginning to trust that gut feeling.

I should have trusted it with that damnable champagne at the celebration. I could have avoided all this. Maybe.

Rogan, the kitchen's head chef, was as hard a sell on a second chance as Myrta had promised. Only when I told him she personally had sent me, singing his praises, did his shoulders ease forward again, his jaw relaxing.

"Fine, newbie. One shot, and one only. You can start by taking Silas's place on dishes from the morning meal, and by Aprella, you'd better not take your time with that."

Before I could thank him, he turned and stormed off to the other end of the castle's huge kitchen, shouting at someone else.

I made my way to the sinks. There, the mountain of dishes was... mountainous. How many people ate at one castle? I sighed and walked up to the guy frantically washing dishes. "Hey, are you Silas?"

He didn't look up. "What do you want? You know, I had to work an hour late last night, and the whole shift got moved from evenings to day shift because you couldn't hack one day in the kitchen. So I ask again, what do you want?"

I waited as he halfway shouted at me, letting him finish his roll. Jericho had taught me that the best way to let others get over my mistakes sometimes was to let them vent. When he finished, I replied, "I know. I was homesick, but I came back and fell on my own sword to Myrta and Chef Rogan. I'm sorry you had to work late because of me."

"Sure did, newbie. So, you feel bad—what's that to me?" He still didn't look up.

"Nothing at all. It's just words. But as far as words go, you have mine that I'll make it up to you. I'll take shifts you don't want, jobs you don't want, whatever. Rogan told me to come take over dishes, for you. Will you let me do that? Please. I want to make it up to you."

Actually, I found I meant every word. It was high time I acted like the Prince of Ochana. I was startled to realize that I really did want to earn a good reputation, not because I had "prince" before my name, but because my word mattered to me. So, when he flung off his dish-washing gloves and strode away, grumbling, I didn't waste time fuming about how he could dare not believe me, or pitying myself for having to earn their acceptance all over again from even farther behind. That was my fault, and I knew it.

Instead, I got busy scrubbing dishes, moving as fast as I could with my Mahier fueling both my speed and my endurance. It was hard work, to be sure, especially since I was trying to impress Rogan, but actually, the work was kind of peaceful. After a while, I just sort of lost track of time, stopped whining about where I was or who I was, and got absorbed in the rhythm of washing dishes. Before I knew it, the morning dishes were done and two hours had gone by judging from the sunlight. I looked around, coming back to reality as Silas walked by.

He stopped, looked between me and the dishes, and gave me a nod before walking off.

Rogan, at the woodstoves, waved me over.

I wound my way between tables and stacks of boxes to where he stood. "Yes, Chef? I'm done with the dishes, ready for whatever you need me for."

"It's about time. But good job. I didn't hear you whine even once. Listen, this Ratatouille is missing something. Wolands might not notice, but I do. Take a taste and tell me what you think."

"Um... Okay. If they won't notice, though, why does it matter?"

Rogan simultaneously pursed his lips and smiled at me. "Because I care about my craft, even when no one else does. Now, taste it."

I picked up a spoon and tasted his dish. It was... delicious. I was about to say so, when a though occurred to me. I was only "feeling" it on part of my tongue. This gave it a flavor that was kind of flat.

My eyebrows furrowed as I thought how to explain it.

"It needs, I don't know, like more depth? Maybe... something citrus, or nutty? Just to fill out the flavor. But it's really good like it is now."

"Really. You stand by that?"

I was about to say no—I wasn't the chef, after all, so what did I know? But that didn't mean I was wrong. "Well, you know better than me, Chef. But for me, I think it needs something else, yeah."

He snapped his fingers and spun to his spice rack. "I thought so too, newbie. Maybe I'll try some coriander seed. It'll add a citrus, nutty edge to warm up the flavor. Well done, kid."

I found myself smiling. Maybe he cared more about making a better dish than he did about getting praise from Wolands, or he'd have just shoved it out the door and called it done. And he hadn't gotten defensive about my criticism but seemed to genuinely appreciate a second opinion. It was all about the craft to him.

Surprisingly, I could understand that feeling. I'd been satisfied with a job well done on the dishes, though no one but these other Galians I worked with would ever appreciate the work I'd done. It was enough just doing something tangible I could take credit for doing well, and cooking involved more creativity than I'd imagined. Who knew? Plus, maybe he'd been testing me for some future task. I could hope. Tasting food all day sounded like a much nicer job than doing stacks of dishes that were taller than me.

I was walking away, going to look for something else

productive to do, when Rogan said, "Hey, kid. We still have lunch to handle and clean up after, but then it's shift change. I don't need you for a couple of days, after that. When we're done here, go do something fun for a couple of days, and I'll see you back here the next morning."

I grinned until he snarled, "Don't just stand there like an idiot. Go peel potatoes. Dinner isn't going to prep itself, kid, and I'd better not see one bit of skin on the pile when you're done."

I saluted him like a soldier, then moved to the alcove where we kept all the potatoes. Three crates of the spuds and a sharp peeler awaited me. But far from groaning about it, I found myself whistling softly as I got to work. Being a Galian wasn't all bad, even if it was hard work and the only people who valued it were other Galians.

Two days off already. Huh. I had little to do and nowhere in particular to do it. Remembering my conversation with Arden about getting in touch with her, I decided to drop off a note to her as we'd discussed. Maybe she would want to spend my days off together or have some ideas about what to do. If not, well, Chef Rogan might take pity on me and let me work, instead. Ha. I'd never preferred working to doing nothing before.

That realization gave me a lot to think about.

CHAPTER 12

Arden hefted one backpack over her shoulders, then handed me the other. "You ready to fly?"

They were high-end packs, the kind with aluminum frames, H-harness shoulder straps, and a padded strap across the belly. Tied to the bottoms with para-cord, each pack had a warm-weather sleeping bag. We'd have to clutch the packs in our talons when we summoned our Dragons, but until then, the frames made them awkward and uncomfortable to wear slung over one shoulder as I usually did. I slid the straps over both shoulders but didn't bother with the belly strap, as she had.

"More than ready. Let's bounce, shall we?"

She laughed as we turned to walk out of the store to head toward the landing pads. "Aprella willing, as my father would say, we don't bounce off anything. Doing so usually means you should have shifted into your Dragon sooner."

It was good to hear someone happy, for once.

She glanced at my pack. "Put on the tummy strap. If you don't, it'll fly off when you go on your little trip."

I did as she suggested without thinking. "You should have seen my boss yesterday. He let me taste what he was cooking and asked my opinion. When's the last time you heard a Leslo ask anyone for their opinion about how to do their job?"

"Or about anything." She frowned. "I'm glad you're finding your way now, given what happened to you, but all our problems will be right here waiting for us when we get back. Let's focus on getting out of here."

Shortly, we arrived at the platforms. Unfortunately, they were pretty busy. Several caravans were arriving, and between the Leslo merchants and their Sien porters, there wasn't much room on the pads, much less a convenient, discreet place to jump off. With caravans delivering, the shields were certainly raised, and the wings were out patrolling. Not the best time to sneak away. We went to a foodie cart and got breakfast while we waited for the caravans to leave, and chatted over a meal, tucked into one of the emptier corners.

By the time we finished eating, they were gone, and we were more than ready to get going. After "the jump," I had expected us to make our way to the cave in Greenland, but instead, she banked west, white scales gleaming in the sun.

We reached land, I think in Canada. After we dropped off the backpacks we'd been clutching in our talons, we spent much of the day flying all over, racing through the forest trees and dive-bombing rabbits in a competition to see who could catch more. Her smaller Dragon was more agile and beat mine in both competitions, but not by much.

It felt good to laugh. It felt even better to just be myself again.

Shortly before the sun went down, we made camp in the woods, far from any settlement, and set our sleeping bags out next to a small lake. We made a bonfire, lit it with dragonfire, and roasted our rabbits over the fire. We'd both worked up quite an appetite flying so much, but we took our time eating. We talked about normal things, not plots and schemes and problems. As the bonfire settled down to coals and low flames, we were lying on our backs, staring up at the stars, spotting constellations, when she rolled over onto her side and propped her head up on one hand. Her expression was inscrutable.

After a moment, I found myself smiling awkwardly. "What? Do I have rabbit on my chin?"

She leveled her gaze at me and slowly shook her head. "This isn't something I tell people, but… I have visions."

"Visions? Like, of grandeur?"

"No, that's delusions. I have visions—I see things. When I was little, I told my real parents—not my biological ones—that I was having daytime dreams, describing the visions, but they just seemed uncomfortable. I was too little to understand why, but I never brought it up again to anyone until now. Back then, you know, I didn't realize magic was real. Now that I know it exists, I have to wonder... Why do I get visions?"

"I don't know." I could see she was troubled, but all I could think to say was, "What kind of visions?"

"Oh, at first, they were just like video clips, images of me flying with dragons. But then, I saw my brother, Trey. I didn't know him then, but I recognized him the first time we met. In that vision, I saw he was going to do something bad at a party. I ignored it... until I saw him hand you that goblet. That's when I realized the vision was about you getting poisoned... and there was nothing I could do to stop it." She looked down at the soft forest floor, eyes narrowed, pursing her lips.

I reached out and took her hand. Maybe the gesture would help her as it had me. "There wasn't anything you could have done. You tried, but really, what else could you have done? That's not your fault, it's Trey's. But have you had other visions? Anything else that hasn't yet happened? It might give us clues."

She squeezed my hand lightly. "The last one I had was when I first arrived in Ochana. I saw a beautiful golden dragon, but that's impossible, right? That's not a color."

"Then again, neither is white, and neither is my rainbow of colors." I smiled.

"Yeah... That's true. Anyway, this beautiful golden Dragon told me, 'It'll all work out in the end.' I have no idea what she meant, but I hope it's about you and all of this."

So did I, and I told her as much.

After a while, we just talked about our human families, and growing up, and our first days in Ochana. We fell asleep still holding hands between our two sleeping bags, mid-conversation.

I slept great.

The next evening, after another day of fun and competitions, we packed up. We cleaned up any sign of our presence before we flew home. I hadn't felt so refreshed in a long time, and I was still full of energy when we landed in Ochana.

We started walking toward her house, chatting about our tree slalom races and catching rabbits, and all too soon, her manor gates loomed ahead of us.

I turned around to face her and regretted having to end our little vacation from reality. "Thanks for coming, Arden. I had fun, and to be honest, I needed that. You're a real friend."

She smiled—then her eyes went wide and clicked to a spot over my shoulder.

I turned my head and found myself looking directly into bright, emerald eyes framed by thin smoke contrails. Umbran's eyes, narrowed and staring into my own.

He spoke in a whisper that sounded louder than any shouting Jericho ever gave me. "I will not have my daughter consorting with the likes of *you*."

"I... We..." I stammered, but couldn't think of anything to say. His eyes were hypnotic. Deer-in-headlights hypnotic.

"Silence. No daughter of mine will be seen with a Sien. I will not abide my daughter slumming it with your kind. If I see you again with her, you will both regret it, I promise you that. Especially you. Am I clear?"

"I... Yes, sir..."

"Good. Now, leave my daughter and get off my estate if you wish to leave at all."

He drilled holes into me with his eyes, and the hairs standing on the back of my neck told me he was deadly serious. I glanced at Arden, but she didn't look up. There was nothing I could do but get out while I still could, but my only thought was to leave before she got into more trouble. Had I just lost my only ally? There was no way things could get any worse, at least.

It wasn't until I was a block away that I realized what he'd said.

"*... a Sien like you ...*"

I'd been wrong. Things had just gotten worse.

CHAPTER 13

I had to go back to work. Blah. My "Monday." Fortunately, Arden and I had risen with the sun while camping for the last few days, so by the time my after-breakfast shift came up, I was already awake and cleaned up. Even better, some snooty Leslo bought me coffee, and though it was probably so he could feel smug about helping someone less fortunate, I thanked him and gave him the "gold star sticker," so to speak, to encourage him to do something like that again in the future with some other less fortunate soul.

After caffeinating, I made my way to the castle kitchens, humming a really old human song, "It's the End of the World as We Know It," by R.E.M.

When I got to the kitchen, however, Myrta was there talking to a red-faced Chef Rogan, and my off-key humming faded when I saw him pounding his fist into his palm, yelling, "I'm telling you, that kid isn't showing up."

"Oh? And how do you know that? I thought you said he had gotten his head screwed on straight and settled into his role."

Chef Rogan's shoulders rolled back, his spine straightening to his full height. "I thought so, but no one has seen him. He didn't have a family hosting him, but he never checked in at the New Dragons hostel. I checked. I'll bet my next soufflé that he ran off to go pretend he's a human."

I took a deep breath, put on a smile, and approached them. "Sorry to disappoint you, Chef, but I'm here for work and ready to go. What should I do first?"

Before Rogan could reply, Myrta snarled, "For Aprella's sake, what are you doing here, Sien? Go to *your* job. This is Galian business."

My smile vanished, and the image of Umbran's angry mistake in calling me a Sien came flooding back. Had it been a mistake, after all? "No, I work here, and—"

Myrta interrupted me again. "Look, kid, I know a whole fleet of you newbies just arrived, but you've been here long enough to know where you're assigned to work. And it sure isn't with the blues in this kitchen."

Deja vu. "But, Myrta, you know me," I said, and I could hear the desperation in my own voice.

Just then, Silas walked by, heading toward the lockers in the back. I stopped him, holding my arm out to block his path. "Silas, tell them I work here. Seriously, the joke has gone far enough."

He stared at me, the corners of his mouth edging slowly downward. "I don't know how you know my name, but even a new Dragon ought to know Siens don't work the kitchens." He shrugged off my hand and continued heading into the back, leaving me standing there with my eyebrows furrowed and my lips pursed. Over his shoulder, he said, "I wouldn't mind having one of you around to carry the potatoes from the warehouse, though."

Myrta let out a heavy sigh. "Listen, newbie, I seriously do not have time for this, and neither does Vini, but it's *her* job to get you straightened out, not mine. Hang on."

She pulled out her cell phone, pressing the button to slide the front cover around to form the keypad, and dialed. I heard it ring twice before someone answered, and Myrta said, "Hey, girl, it's Myrta ... Yeah, business, unfortunately ... We got a problem, or actually, you do. One of your newbies is at the castle kitchens, confused about where Siens should be working. He must really want to work here, because he tried convincing us he had been assigned here. Was that your doing?"

The voice on the other end grew loud enough for me to hear. I couldn't make out the words, but her tone told me everything I needed to know.

Myrta frowned, and a moment later, she closed the phone cover and looked at me again. "Okay, she's on the way. Go wait by the door and stay out of everyone's way until *your* handler gets here."

I just stared at her. This couldn't be happening. Not again. I was silver now? Really? The Fates may have been on my side when we crushed the Time of Fear, but now that the prophecy had been fulfilled, I was quickly coming to the conclusion that I did not like them anymore. I trudged over to the door to wait, muttering curses at the Fates under my breath.

In under five minutes, a rather thin, muscular woman flung the door open and almost walked right by me until she gave me a passing glance—and came to an abrupt halt. She glared at me, eye to eye. "You're the new Sien, right? The troublemaker. For Aprella's sake, what are you doing here?"

"I work here—"

"No, you don't. I don't know who put you up to this gag, but it's not funny. I'm far too busy to babysit a bunch of new Dragons pulling practical jokes, do you understand?"

I just looked away. Today had clearly turned into some kind of waking nightmare, another one of *those* days. "Yes, ma'am. Where do you need me?"

She stared for a long moment, eyes roaming my face, but then her shoulders slumped, and she sighed. "I appreciate your attitude, not giving me a hard time like you did Myrta and Chef Rogan. Look, I know it's hard being new, and I'm guessing you and your friends thought this would lighten things a bit. Am I right?"

She didn't wait for my reply before pulling out her cell

phone to type something on the keypad, grumbling. After a moment, she looked me in the eyes. "We need you to go work in the fields at one of our farms, where we grow vegetables for everyone in Ochana, not only Wolands and Leslos. That makes it doubly important to do the best you can, but if you do well there, we'll see about moving you somewhere else. Here, take a look at my phone."

She showed me a map, with a route traced to a spot not so far from the castle, just on the other side of a Sien and Galian neighborhood. I tried to thank her, but she scooted me out the door, not listening.

I could only stare as she went back inside. Then, I made my way to the place she'd shown me on the map. At the gates, a foreman of some sort greeted me tersely and handed me a basket with a pair of new leather work gloves inside. "Here. You'll be picking the red fruits in the east field."

As I made my way out there, I saw others working. Some took their fully laden baskets to some kind of machine and dumped them in, then turned around to go back out to the field.

I followed their example. I didn't know what else to do. I also didn't know how to cut the unrecognizable produce, but one showed me how to cut what turned out to be peppers, and he showed me how to dump them so they didn't get bruised. Then, I sort of lost myself in the repetitive monotony of it all. Clip, stuff, carry, dump, repeat. It was hard work, and by the end of the day, my Mahier had been nearly drained just keeping me going. I worked for hours, and when a whistle sounded, everyone immediately headed toward the machine to dump whatever they had. Again, I followed their example.

In spite of using magic to keep my muscles fueled and the lactic acid from burning too much, I was exhausted. It was beyond me how anyone could do that job every day, all day, year after year.

I did that job for three more days, each night trudging to the hostel for new Dragons to pass out, only to be awoken at dawn for breakfast... and more produce picking.

On the fourth day, however, near the end of my shift, the foreman waved me over to the machine where we dumped our baskets. I came over with a half-full basket and dumped what I had. "Yes, sir?"

"You've done good. You pull your weight. So, why don't you go with the delivery team and bring today's haul into town? It all goes to warehouses by the Woland barracks. It'll be a nice, easy last couple of hours for your shift, eh?"

I found myself smiling for the first time in days. "Yes, sir. Thanks! I appreciate it."

"Yeah, yeah. Get your silver rear end in gear, kid—we don't got all day." He smiled, then strode away to yell at someone else for some real or imagined mistake. Probably breathing wrong, but that was their problem. I was just glad not to be gathering vegetables for a few hours.

I hopped into the truck's passenger seat and the driver immediately pulled out with two other trucks following behind. On the way, the driver kept up a slow monologue about farming, but mercifully, it was a short trip, and we soon pulled into a parking lot at a large warehouse. I recognized the place, surrounded by barracks buildings. I had zero wish to see any red Dragons at the moment, but I also couldn't wait to end the monologue coming from the driver, so I practically vaulted out of the truck cab to start unloading.

An armed and armored Woland stomped up to me, steam trickling from his nose. "You, Sien."

I looked up—and froze. I knew that Dragon. "Arch?"

The Dragon cocked her head, lip curling back, and grabbed my shirt. "Yeah, you can read a name-tape. Congratulations, silver. Follow me."

She turned to leave, but I made no move to follow. I just looked back and forth between Arch and my driver, not sure what to do.

Arch's eyes flared a pale red. "Did I stutter, maggot? There's a mess in my quarters, and I don't have time to clean it *and* drill *and* pass inspections, so get your lazy rear in there and grab a mop."

When I again didn't move, she rounded on me and stared down, directly into my eyes. "Did I stutter, Sien, or are you just stupid? You. Grab mop. Clean. My room. *Move it.*"

"But, Arch, I have to unload..." My voice trailed away as I saw more Wolands I recognized from the wing approaching. They did not look happy.

They stopped in a half-circle around me, half a step farther than Arch. Eyes glowed, smoke flowed.

Arch growled at me. "Sien, I don't care if you're here to cut King Rylan's hair, I told you to get to my quarters and clean. I'm going to give you to the count of three before I start to feel awfully disrespected, boy."

I found myself stepping backward, away from the angry-looking soldiers who suddenly looked alien to me. "I..."

I glanced at my partner again, but he merely stood back, eyes downcast, hands hanging limply. I'd get no help from him, it seemed. Well, mopping a floor wasn't any harder than unloading a truck, and I was beyond outnumbered as Arch's eyes glowed brighter by the moment. Oh well...

I looked down. "Okay, ma'am. Which room am I cleaning?" Oof. Saying that felt almost as bad as a kick to my gut.

"Wise choice, silver." She spun on her heels and strode away, and I fell into step behind her, flanked on either side by her wing-mates in case I got any bright ideas about running I supposed.

I made no attempt to get away.

We passed two intersecting hallways, then turned and stopped at the next door on the left. A Woland flung the door open, and Arch—I think it was her, at least—shoved me through the doorway and said, "Mop and broom are in the closet by the lavatory. The mess is between bunks *3* and *4*, but get the whole floor. If I step on a piece of glass, I'm looking you up, *Sien*."

Before I could reply, she and the other Wolands marched out in lockstep and headed down the hallway.

Sigh.

I looked around the barracks and pursed my lips. The mess between bunks 3 and 4 wasn't a small thing. No, that was really more like the epicenter of devastation, which spread halfway across the barracks room. The floor was drenched and sparkled from glass fragments of what looked like several shattered cups. Two trash cans lay flung across the floor, along with their contents. One of the two foot-lockers at the end of the bunks was overturned, its contents covered in glass, water, and trash.

"What the hell kind of hurricane hit this place?" Briefly, I thought of just leaving. But then I realized that cleaning up here was still better than offloading a hundred heavy crates of produce, so I went to the closet to grab the mop and broom and got busy cleaning. After I picked up all the trash that was big enough to easily grab, I shook off the individual items from the footlocker to get as much glass and muck off her uniform items, notebooks, and more.

As I swept more glass, I accidentally hit the footlocker with the broom, making it pivot slowly on its slightly bowed bottom. A scrap of paper emerged as the chest spun. I leaned down to grab the trash, but what came up in my hand wasn't trash. It was a photograph.

I gingerly wiped it off, revealing the beaming, gorgeous smile of a young woman. Not just any woman, this one was beautiful and vivacious. Someone had drawn a heart on the picture in felt-tip marker.

She looked familiar, actually. Considering it, I tapped my chin for a moment, and then it came to me—she was another new Dragon I'd met at the farm. A Sien named Lelah. The name written below the heart confirmed it.

I tucked the photo into the footlocker carefully as I finished cleaning the barracks. I closed the door to the Wolands' room with only one thought on my mind: *Why would a Woland soldier have a photo of a Sien?*

CHAPTER 14

I had the next day off, but Arden never picked up the note I dropped through the Sepens manor's fence. I was a bit worried, but my plan of lurking outside to watch for her was foiled by a Woland guard at the neighboring estate who, in no uncertain terms, let me know I should move along. I checked again that evening, but the note was still there, so I reached in and grabbed it. No point leaving evidence she'd never see.

In the morning, I returned to the farm. I spotted Lelah a couple times, but our jobs left me no opportunity to cross her path. As I kept working, my thoughts weren't on Lelah, though, but Arden. I didn't think her father would harm her, but who knew what imprisonment he might have meted out to "protect" her from the dangerous, wily silver Dragon?

I was working on picking my fourth bushel when

another Dragon, after dumping a full basket into the combine, paused as they passed me going the other way. I looked up, curious, but waited for him to speak first.

After a moment, he said, "There's a young woman here to see you, kid. Said her name was Arden."

I almost dropped my basket and looked around. "Where is she, and where's the foreman?"

He smiled. "The foreman says 'it's all remiges and rectrices'—that means you can go ahead, I think—but he said you'd better not fall behind. She's by the combine truck." He nodded his chin to indicate the drop-off truck behind me.

I walked briskly, dodging other workers, and then spotted Arden leaning against the giant front bumper on the combine. "Oh, what a sight for sore eyes you are. I'm glad you came. You okay?"

But instead of smiling and nodding, she didn't meet my gaze. She shook her head. "No, I'm pretty far from okay. I've been thinking about this for a couple of days now, and I've come to a decision."

I forced my smile to stay painted on my face. "Oh? We're eloping?"

That brought a faint smile back, at least. She shrugged. "That wouldn't be the worst thing for me, but you have to stay here. You have a duty and a life to get back. Me? I'm... To be honest, I'm afraid of my father and Trey. They haven't hurt me, but what would they do if they knew who you were? Look at what they did to you already. If my father would do this to you just to further his own ends, I don't feel very safe in my own home."

My eyes went so wide that they hurt. "You? Afraid of your father? I don't know what to say. Uh, do you have a hideout besides the cave? I mean, a place to go and lie low, away from your family?"

She ran one hand through her long hair, brushing it out of the way, but one lock fell back, hiding half her face. "Yes, I'm going back to the ground. I can't stay in Ochana anymore, I just can't."

I nodded. Her options here in Ochana were rather limited, and I couldn't blame her. "Will you stay with your old host family?"

"My humans? Goodness, no. I would love to—don't misunderstand me—but they knew I was a Dragon the whole time, yet they never told me. I had to find out when I freaked out about smoke coming out of my nose."

"Then, where? I wish I knew a place for you."

"I've heard of a place where Dragons who don't like Ochana can go, where we can live our own lives, not because of some stupid color chart." She looked over her shoulder, to both sides, and everywhere but at me for a moment. Then, in almost a whisper, she replied, "It's a place called *Sanctuary*."

I stared at her, my thoughts racing in a jumble as I recalled the conversation I overhead when I'd been helping Siens clear the riot damage. So, Sanctuary was a place, one she somehow knew about. It was real… I didn't have to go through all this. I could escape, start looking for a real solution to my problem. "I've heard of it. Do you know—"

Arden's eyes flared a blindingly bright white light. She rose up off of the ground, hanging limply, but her mouth opened into an O-shape. Words tumbled out, though her mouth didn't move. The voice that came out of her echoed and shifted from a woman's voice to a man's and back again.

"The Time of Fear has passed, and yet the flames of war come anew. It is a pyre, burning away love and all that is decent. Dragon turns upon Dragon, brother upon brother, daughter upon father, and in the end, all is undone. Two alone stand beyond the machinations of those who seek Ochana's undoing—the Keeper of Dragons, She of Pearl and He of All-Hues. Only the Keeper can prevent the end of our world."

The light in Arden's eyes grew so bright that it hurt to look at her, then vanished as suddenly as it had come, and she collapsed into my arms, sweat beading on her forehead. I didn't know what to do. All I could do was cradle her head and lower her to the ground as gently as I could as I called her name over and over.

CHAPTER 15

When Arden opened her eyes, she seemed confused, blinking rapidly and looking around. "What happened? Get off me, you goof."

I helped her regain her balance, then stepped back. "It looked like something took over your body. They had a message, too. A war is coming, one that will turn Dragons against each other. Only 'she of pearl' and 'he of many hues' can stop it. Sounds like you and me since, you know, the message was for us."

She furrowed her eyebrows, looking down. "Something took over me? I guess I believe you. I feel like I'm still putting my body back on, like a coat... But, I'm not sure that's our problem, Cole."

"What do you mean?" I stared, disbelieving. "How is this

anyone's problem but ours? We can't just turn our back on Ochana."

She reached out to brush her fingertips across my cheek, smiling wanly. "Cole, look around. Ochana turned its back on us, not the other way around. Whatever magic is at work here, you've seen what it's like for Galians and Siens. Before that, you saw how the Wolands are used by Leslos, not like partners, but like just another tool—a bludgeon to keep the other tools in line. Is it worth saving?"

I… I wasn't sure how to answer that. She was right, and I realized I wasn't all that excited about the opportunity to suffer a lot more to save a system I'd now seen from both sides. And yet… "Arden, look, I know the system sucks. It's not what I would have envisioned as a human if someone had told me there was a mythical realm of noble Dragonkind."

"Kind of my point, Cole."

I nodded but said, "The war that's coming will kill a lot of people. It'll end Ochana. It'll end the Dragons as a people, if not as a species."

She frowned and looked away.

I kept going. "We can't just stand by and let that happen, because all the war I've seen so far tells me that the ones who suffer most are the innocent people who are just trying to get by. Siens and Galians will get the worst of it, I think, but the red and green Dragons don't seem to realize that Ochana stands or falls on the backs of the silvers and blues."

Her eyes welled up, and she blinked rapidly before

wiping one eye. "Cole, what can we do? Seriously, how can two Dragons make any difference? If you come up with something real, something tangible, I'll think about it. But in the meantime, I'm going to keep looking for Sanctuary. When I find it, I'll get in touch with you."

It was my turn to blink, surprised. "You don't want to see me until then? Why? We need to talk and plan and… I don't know. Do things to stop this."

"Right, but until we have an escape plan, we can't be seen together. I think my father must be the cause of what's coming, don't you?"

"Well… yeah. It must be him, I'm sorry to say."

"Right. And if he's willing to go that far, he won't hesitate to hurt you to keep me away from you. If a war really is coming—and I don't doubt you, from what I've seen with my own eyes—then you being seen with me could make you his first victim of the war. Understand? It could set off the very war we're supposed to stop."

I didn't want to agree, but she could be right. We had no idea what would set it off. "I guess caution is the best approach. I don't like it, though."

"Me either. Look, listen, keep alert. Maybe the Fates will present us with some way to stop the war. In the meantime, like I said, I'll look for Sanctuary, and I'll contact you when I have something to tell you. For now, though, we have to go back to our lives. Act like nothing's up, okay? Don't give anyone a good reason to focus on you. I think we're already in dangerous times."

We parted ways, plans changed. I had work in the morning, and I wasn't in much of a mood to just hang out anywhere. Impending doom took any joy out of that idea. Instead, I headed back to my lodging and went to bed early.

The next day, on my way to work, a Woland checkpoint stood in my way. They put Siens and Galians through a metal detector before letting us continue. Leslos and Wolands, though, were waved around the checkpoint. It made me a couple of minutes late for work, and when I checked in with the foreman, he was grumpier than usual, yelling at me and a few others who had been made late. Behind him, a Woland stood with crossed arms, but he wasn't watching us—he stared at the foreman, watching his every move.

At lunch, I found another checkpoint at the lunch wagons, again putting us through metal detectors. I couldn't help but join the other Siens in grumbling about the intrusion. It took up almost half of my lunch break, and when the bell rang to warn of lunch's end, the Wolands immediately got busy chasing the Siens out of the sitting area.

After work, the first checkpoint had been expanded to check everyone going in *both* directions—everyone who happened to be a Sien or Galian, at least.

The next day, I left for work ten minutes earlier, and I'd bought a meal the night before to bring for lunch in a backpack. At lunch, I joined Lelah and many of the others from my work site, eating on the farm instead of going to the foodie wagons. Everyone around me was unusually quiet, conversing in a whisper. Red Dragons standing nearby watching us were a big part of that.

Halfway through our lunch break, the Woland touched his finger to his ear, nodded, and said something I couldn't hear. He ran north, out of view. Only once he was gone did the conversation grow louder than a whisper.

One of the others, glaring at the Woland's retreating back, said, "Lelah, did you have any trouble getting through the riot this morning?"

Riot? What riot? I looked at Lelah, awaiting her reply.

She said, "No, I didn't. I went around it. We got word about it from a runner, so we avoided it. I saw some of the damage, though. It would have taken a lot of us to make that much damage."

The other Sien nodded. "Well, there's ten times as many of us as there are of those damnable Wolands. I'm glad you didn't have any trouble, though. I heard there's another riot planned tonight, in District Eight."

She shook her head, frowning. "Another one? Why, this time?"

The other shrugged. "We're tired of getting yanked off the street after work to go do more work for the Leslos, I guess. As if working twelve hours a day isn't enough. Bah." Smoke drifted up from his nostrils.

Lelah's, too. "Well, if they tried that with me, I'd fight

back, too. It's not right. How much more are they going to ask of us?"

The grumbling all around mirrored my own thoughts, and it was all I could do to keep smoke from *my* nostrils. But fighting armed and armored Wolands in the streets wasn't a recipe for success.

I whispered to Lelah, "I'll walk with you after work. Stay out of those fights, okay? I don't want you getting hurt, and I've seen what Wolands can do in a real fight."

I walked her home, but we had to go around two separate blocks, filled with smoke and cordoned off by Wolands.

Two days after Arden's visit and frightening episode, I left my quarters early to meet Lelah near her home and walked to work with her and a couple of other young Siens. Rather than going straight to work, however, Lelah took us a block out of the way, where we joined up with another small group of Siens. Safety in numbers, she explained, and I didn't argue. Ten of us were certainly safer than one, or two, or even five.

A new Woland checkpoint stood between us and the farm, though. The older Dragons among us grumbled, but we all got in line. It was best to just blend in, and I wasn't carrying anything to raise concerns. Standing with the others and waiting for our turns, however, I noticed something different about the red Dragons running the checkpoint. On their armored arms, they had Ochana's symbol etched on the shoulder, as usual, but beneath that, they wore a new symbol. Freshly etched, larger for the leaders especially, but all the rank-and-file red Dragons there also had it.

The symbol of House Sepens.

A car with flags on the bulbous hood—someone important—drove up to the checkpoint. I squinted to see who would get out, but when the driver emerged, I gasped. "Jericho?"

Lelah nudged me. "You know him? He's the most powerful Woland around, just about. Where do you know him from?"

I hurried over to Jericho without answering her, moving as quickly as I could without drawing attention, hoping to get close before the checkpoint Wolands intercepted me.

But rough hands grabbed my shoulders from behind when I was twenty feet away.

I shouted, "Jericho, it's me, Cole. We have to talk!"

But as the Woland guardian dragged me back to the line, Jericho spotted me, and for a moment, my hopes rose.

Then, he turned away to talk to the checkpoint's commander.

Yeah, he didn't recognize me. Of course. "Damn"

The Woland shoved me into line hard enough that I almost fell over. "Watch your mouth with me, Sien."

He spun away before I could think of a reply.

The other Siens dusted me off and got me balanced on

my feet again. One muttered profanity at the Woland in an uninterrupted and rather creative stream.

When I got up to the checkpoint gate, I saw Lelah off to one side with some other Siens, but before I got the chance to ask her what was going on, the Woland who had shoved me stepped up and thrust one finger into my chest, baring his teeth at me in a predator's grin. "This one will do. Put him with the others."

"Wait, where are you—"

Another red Dragon grabbed my arm and goose-stepped me to Lelah's group. He didn't answer my questions, either.

When he was out of earshot, Lelah moved to stand beside me. She whispered, "We're going with some Galians, too."

"Where?"

She paused before answering. "We're being sent to Umbran Sepens' estate. He's got a party coming up. We get the privilege of setting it up."

I already had a notion of what the working conditions would be like. The hair on the backs of my arms stood on end. Just perfect.

CHAPTER 16

Under the noonday sun, I was just as sweaty from the work as the other Siens. Putting up the pavilions and gazebos was harder work than I'd expected. I looked with a bit of envy at the Galians who were merely handling decorations and wiped my brow with my sleeve. I had a new appreciation for the kitchen work I'd done when they all thought I was a blue Dragon.

A couple other Siens and I raised a heavy wooden wall. Once we got it upright, others secured it with ropes on both sides to keep it that way. The assembly looked like it would become some sort of miniature barn. Hay bales were stacked to the side, adding to the impression. Umbran seemed to be going with some sort of country-chic style, for his party.

I smirked, imagining Umbran in cowboy boots and a diamond-encrusted cowboy hat, but as I turned to get the next part, I almost ran into someone standing right behind me. I looked behind me, but all I saw were a pair of glowing, green eyes narrowed menacingly. I recognized those eyes immediately.

Umbran Sepens stared back at me.

Hastily, I stammered, "Mister Sepens, I..."

"Silence," he hissed. "Do not speak to me, Sien. Where is my daughter?"

"What?" I froze, desperately trying to figure out why he had asked and how I could answer without speaking to him. My thoughts were all adrenaline and confusion. My gaze was locked onto his like a deer in headlights. The sounds of work all around me stopped, though whether it was because the others were watching us or because my heart was pounding in my ears, I wasn't sure.

"I'll ask this one more time. Where. Is. Arden?" His menace was palpable. I was on his property, surrounded by Wolands wearing his patch on their arms.

I blurted, "I haven't even seen your daughter, sir. Why would I know that?"

Behind him, Siens began picking up tools, and the Wolands—outnumbered ten-to-one—slid hands to weapons. Why I saw that with crystal clarity, I don't know, but it gave me strength. My people weren't going to let me get yanked and "disappeared" by this guy.

Umbran didn't seem to notice, though. He took a step toward me. "Listen here, you little—"

A Sien nearby coughed loudly. "Sir, the young man was

pretty clear. His question is valid. Why would your daughter be caught dead slumming around with a Sien, Mister Sepens? Our kind is beneath her."

Umbran seemed to notice the situation around him for the first time and blinked twice, surprised. He leaned in closer, and said almost under his breath, "If I find out you know where she is and didn't tell me, an army of your Sien trash-mates won't save you, boy."

He strode away, his shoulder knocking into mine as he passed me. He went straight to a waiting car, and it drove off as soon as he was inside.

I breathed a sigh of relief, as I'm sure everyone else did, too. Work resumed, though the Wolands kept a bit greater distance after that.

At lunch, we were scattered around the work zone, as only a few had left to get lunch at the foodie trucks outside the gate, dealing with the pat-downs and metal detectors. Lelah found me and sat beside me and a few other Siens on a big, ornamental rock. She only nibbled at her sandwich, though, while the rest of us devoured half a dozen each.

Halfway through lunch, I finally asked her, "What's wrong? You're not eating much."

She pushed her sandwich away, then looked around before she replied. "I don't like the way the Sepens son and some of the others staying at the house look at me. I don't feel... I don't know. Safe."

I felt the smoke coming from my nostrils, and the silver haze around everything I looked at told me my eyes were glowing. I closed my eyes and took a deep breath, then said, "Stay close to me, Lelah. No one will do anything to you if you're never alone."

"Agreed," said another Sien, nodding. "We're all here for you. I'm done letting those reds push us around. But Lelah, isn't your sister a Woland? Maybe you could talk to her about what's going on."

She shook her head, faintly. "She visited me a few times when I was on the ground, before I knew I was a Dragon. My parents said she was a cousin of some sort. But once I summoned my Dragon, and it wasn't red or green, she stopped seeing me."

I could almost feel the hurt coming from her, and slid my hand to her arm. Nothing I could have said would make that better, so I didn't try. She and I spent the rest of our lunch break in silence.

After lunch, when all the new pathways had been set up and most of the work was done, my team started on the gazebos. They were arrayed in a semi-circle around the little barn we'd erected. Most of the other teams were tasked with carrying decorations and such for the Galian workers.

Almost a dozen of us were making quick work of the main structure on the first gazebo when we ran into a problem. Our team foreman was digging through toolboxes and piles of parts, looking for something.

After I finished ratcheting down the last bolt on an upright beam, I approached him. "What's wrong, boss?"

She frowned. "I can't find the tool we'll need to lock down the top cone on this ridiculous thing. It's a little T-shaped tool with a special socket at the end, about the size of an Allen wrench. Have you seen it?"

I shook my head. "Maybe it's with the last pile of gazebo pieces we piled up this morning?"

"Maybe. Go look, would you? I need to double check the torsion on the bolts we already set up."

"Sure thing." I headed to the far side of the party field. There, a gazebo's base had been set, but the other parts stood in piles around it. I climbed up onto the base and started looking through the piles of bolts when I heard someone talking in a low murmur.

I looked around but saw no one. I followed the voice, which was joined by another. They sounded familiar. When I got to a seven-foot pile of half-built components, I recognized them. Umbran and Trey. I moved to the pile's edge and focused my Mahier, magically enhancing my hearing, though not as much as I amplified their voices so I didn't pick up on too many others.

"... worry too much, son. As far as anyone knows, he doesn't even have an heir." Umbran's voice.

Trey replied, "But he's their king. I'm worried they won't allow it. You know that, if they all rise together, there's little we can do to stop them from bringing us down."

Umbran chuckled and said, "That's one worry we don't have. Do you see how divided we've made them? Siens blaming Galians blaming Wolands. They aren't going to risk their lives over the power-plays of a few Leslos. Those same Leslos have allowed things to become as they are, standing by while the rest of us, who value our traditional roles, got busy restoring the natural order of things."

"True... They're rioting in the streets. Leslos are afraid, just as you said they'd be."

A low rumble emitted from Umbran, riding behind his words as he replied, "Then trust me, the rest will go just as I said, as well. When we depose Rylan, no one is going to lift one talon to help him. He let this happen, after all. There's a proper order to things, and Rylan and his father before him messed it all up."

"Too true, Father. Half the Leslos *want* us there."

"Right. Bringing back the old ways. Someone's got to do it, and it fell on us. Take advantage of it while we can, Trey. Soon, the title of Heir to the Throne is going to be right where it always should have been—on the Sepens family. Now come, we have work to do."

I used Mereum to hide myself from their view, despite how much more Merfolk magic it took to do so than if I'd used Dragon magic, but it prevented anyone from sensing heavy Mahier being used so nearby. I needn't have bothered, though, because they walked toward the manor together without so much as a glance behind the stacked gazebo parts.

I found the tool the foreman needed and hurried back to the job at hand with my heartbeat thudding in my ears.

CHAPTER 17

After work, I left with the first crew out of there. I had no intention of still being there with just a few other silver Dragons, especially if Umbran returned. I did my best to blend in and disappear, sticking with them as we hit the food trucks for dinner. Over a meal, I asked to borrow a cell phone and logged into my Dragon-Tools account. Ha, magic could make me disappear, but it hadn't erased everything. I tried to track Arden's phone, but it was either offline or hidden. Next, I checked Jericho's schedule. As I suspected, he would soon be on his way to the daily debriefing with his staff at the barracks.

I logged out and deleted my info before returning the phone, ate quickly, then headed out. The walk wasn't far, even choosing a route that kept me away from the areas I knew had recently rioted—or were rioting. Nonetheless, I had to go through three checkpoints along the way, but the bored-looking Wolands with their dual arm badges were looking for weapons, not specifically to hassle workers. My sword wasn't on me and hadn't been since I stopped being the Prince, so they let me on through.

I hurried past intermittent, light riot damage, even so far from the epicenters.

When I arrived at the barracks, it was easy to see Jericho's flagged car pulling in, and I walked briskly in that direction, trying to get as close as I could without drawing undo attention to myself. As I drew nearer, Jericho climbed out of the back seat. He looked tired, with deep bags under his eyes, and I'd never seen his shoulders slump like that before. In contrast, he might as well have been hunched over.

"Honorable Jericho," I said when I got within earshot.

He spun, his hand moving to his sword hilt, but then relaxed. His eyes stayed narrowed, however. "Yes, citizen?"

I'd known it was too much to hope that he'd recognize me this time when he hadn't before. Oh well. "Sir, I overheard disturbing information while working today at the Sepens estate. I think—"

"Look, you're new. I can see that." He eyed me up and down. "But being a new Sien is no reason to interrupt my schedule. It's rude, and there's a chain of command."

"Yes, sir, but I think you should hear this." I took a breath to continue, but he didn't let me.

"You *think* you have information? Look, kid, I get that

this wasn't the best time ever to discover you're a silver Dragon, but you're going to have a far easier time fitting into all this if you learn the local rules. Follow them, and you'll be fine. I don't have time for this."

I started to take another step toward him, unthinking. "But, sir—"

Two of his entourage stepped between me and Jericho, and one said, "The general was clear. Step away, son, while you can."

They were burly, and armored, and I took a step backward.

Jericho was already walking, heading inside, but those two kept themselves between us until he passed through the doorway and out of sight. As they turned to follow, one said, "I wouldn't try to follow him in there if I were you."

I didn't argue. I stuck my hands in my pockets and walked away defeated.

I didn't really have anywhere to be, and I found myself headed north along the boulevard, in the general direction of Mount Ochana rising up in the distance. I had almost reached my old wing's barracks when I saw a familiar figure emerge from behind some shrubs to approach a couple Dragon guardians standing around, clearly off-duty. It was Lelah, I realized with a start.

A small group of Siens hung back by the bushes. I looked at the other dragons, and sure enough, one of them was Arch. The moment she saw her approaching, her face contorted like she had been hit by a sudden stomach virus.

She performed a crisp about-face, spinning on her heel, and marched inside.

The Dragon she had been chatting with placed himself squarely in the middle of the sidewalk between Lelah and Arch, leaving her no choice but to stop in her tracks. She turned around, hunched over, and walked back to the other Siens, wiping her eyes with her sleeves. As unhappy as Arch had looked, she still wasn't going to give her own damn sister the time of day.

The thought struck me, then… What in Aprella's name was wrong with this place? Ochana wasn't the shining beacon of those who stood for protecting all the Races of Truth that I had been told it was. It was no different than Earth. In fact, it *was* different—it was *worse*. People I had respected, even admired, were content to stand by and watch half of their own kind being treated worse than any mere employee, happy to watch families split apart, too cowardly to stand up for what was right. Most didn't even know what was right but actively embraced the hypocrisy.

Really, what the hell was I fighting for? The thought staggered me. Trying to catch my breath, I turned and headed back toward my quarters, heedless of the route I took. What did it matter, after all?

It didn't matter. The sole reason for this place to exist was as a home for Dragons, but it had become "home" for fewer than half of us. For the rest of us, shining Ochana was just a tarnished memory.

Sanctuary couldn't be worse than this place. By the time

I made it back to my quarters after passing through another couple of checkpoints that were only checking my kind, I had come to a decision. I was going to leave this place to sink in its own hypocrisy. I was going to Earth to be with Arden, following my heart as my father had often told me since I arrived in Ochana.

The thought of leaving all of this brought the first genuine smile to my face that entire day.

CHAPTER 18

It turned out to be rather simple to find the Sien whom I first overheard talking about Sanctuary. The powers-that-be kept meticulous logs of each worker Dragon's prior job locations just in case one of them messed up and needed to be held accountable. All I had to do was walk back to the address where I had encountered them tearing down riot-burned houses, then search for that address. When I found a day with three Siens working "deconstruction," I knew I had the right ones. I wrote their names down, then borrowed another silver Dragon's cell phone to look the first one up. As it turned out, his house wasn't far, and it was his day off. Only one day off, I observed bitterly.

His name was Mike Dolan, and his house was only a

small studio apartment crammed in among twenty others just like it. The landscaping, if you could call it that, was of dingy river stones rather than any pretty, growing things. Cheaper to maintain.

I knocked on his front door, picking a spot with the least peeling paint. I recognize the man who answered, one of the workers from that day. He looked around nervously, then focused on me. "Yes?"

I said, "You won't remember me, but we met a while back while you were tearing down a house that got burned in one of the early riots. You mentioned something, that day, a certain place. It's a place I'd like to get to. I need sanct—"

He cut me off. "Not out here. Come inside, for Aprella's sake."

I followed him inside. Unsurprisingly, it looked as dingy and poor as the outside. He kept it tidy, though. He motioned for me to have a seat on his sleeper couch, currently in couch mode, then leaned against the wall between his tiny kitchen and, well, the rest of the studio.

He stared at me for a long moment, but at last, he said, "So, why should I trust you?"

It was a direct question, and I resolved to give him a direct answer. "I've had it with Ochana. I've had it with being treated like I don't matter by people who don't understand why that's wrong. I've had it with doing all the work to support a privileged few and getting spit on for doing it. When I met you, I thought I could change things. I thought

I could make a difference. But now I see that nothing I do will ever change this place. So, I want to leave. I can't go back to my human family, and wouldn't if I could. I just want out."

Mike leaned his head back to rest it on the wall and covered his face with both hands, dragging them downward as he let out a long, harsh breath. "Oh, man. Well, your timing is great. I've kind of come to the same conclusion as you. This place isn't worth saving, and I wouldn't know how to, even if it were. I've decided to go to Sanctuary, too. It occurs to me that it might be easier for us to get out of here if we work together. You can come with me if you want."

I didn't even have to think about how to answer. It was the whole reason I was there. "Absolutely. When do we leave?"

Nodding, Mike replied, "Yeah, that's the thing. I can't leave tonight. Gotta get some of my affairs in order before I go. I'm leaving in three days. If you want to come, meet me here then, after you get off shift. Then, you and I can escape together. I have to tell you, I'm looking forward to starting over in a better place."

"Thanks. I'll be here." I paused, considering how to phrase my question, but decided just to ask it plainly. "Why would you bring me, though?"

Mike scratched his chin for a moment before replying. "I don't know. You know of Sanctuary, you're unhappy here—that's clear even to a dunce like me—and maybe most importantly, you're a silver Dragon. We have to take care of one another, because no one else will, not even the Galians. They're too busy licking the Leslos' boots for table scraps to take much of a stand, though individuals certainly have stood by us in the riots. But that's as far as they go. Starting over in Sanctuary is going a lot farther than a few joining our riot down the block, so to speak. It's a leap of faith, almost. I'm happy to have others like me at my side when I take that leap."

That, at least, I could understand.

I left Mike Dolan's house feeling much better. We'd talked over snacks, and he was a great guy, just tired of the caste system like I was. To be fair, I hadn't even noticed it before. It bothered me that I'd been blind to it, or at least to its extent, but with the Sepens pushing for a return to some outdated, obsolete nostalgic system that put them firmly at the top, it was impossible to miss anymore. But it had been there even before the Sepens made it so.

I had my way out, though, and this screwy world of Dragons and their politics would soon be behind me. It wasn't like I'd known this world all that long, and having my eyes opened felt like a punch to the gut. Sanctuary was going to feel like my first unfettered breath after having the wind knocked from me. I couldn't wait, and as I turned onto the street, I almost felt like skipping, or running. Something.

"Cole?" A woman's voice behind me made me stop.

It took half a second to place it, and I knew before turning around who it'd be. "Lelah? You following me?"

I turned and saw it was indeed her. She wore a long, dark-colored coat with a deep hood and sneakers. "Yes, actually. I thought you were up to something, but I wanted to see for myself."

"I'm not up to anything," I replied as evenly as I could, though my heart felt like it was fit to burst from my chest, it was beating so fast. "Just saying hi to a guy I met on the job awhile back, that's all." I narrowed my eyes at her. "Now, why are you following me, Lelah? The real truth would be nice."

At first, she stared at me with narrowed eyes, an expression that reminded me of her father. Maybe she knew? No, she couldn't have. Even if she suspected, what could she say? To whom? I could think of no way for her to actually harm me or my plan. She couldn't have more than a suspicion, after all, so I met her gaze and held it.

After a few seconds, though, she seemed to crumple in on herself, shoulders slouching and eyes downcast. They were welling with tears, I noticed, and I had to resist the sudden urge to reach out to comfort her.

She wiped her eyes with her sleeve but still didn't look back up at me. "I want to go with you. I hate it here. All of it, every bit. I hate my sister. I hate this stupid city. I hate how the color of your scales matters more than who you are inside, and no matter what I do, I'll never be a Leslo, so I won't ever matter. I was going to go to college," she said, finally looking up with red-rimmed eyes. "When I thought I was a regular human, I was on my way. I'd have had a life, Cole. I want my life back. My *human* life."

I couldn't think of a better way to try to score points with a cold-hearted sister than to turn in Dragons fleeing to Sanctuary, but I also couldn't very well show up to my rendezvous with Mike with some unknown woman by my side. He'd lose his nerve for sure, and then Lelah and I would both be stuck here, even if she was being honest with me.

All those thoughts flooded me in an instant, and I heard myself say, louder than I should have, "No, Lelah. You can't run from your problems. This is your home now. Maybe not forever, though. I'm going to keep trying to fix all of this. But until I do, you have to bide your time and get by, just like everyone else." I felt dirty just for saying it.

She stared at me wide-eyed, like I'd just spat in her face. In a way, I suppose I had. The tears welled up again, but she didn't seem to notice them this time. "So, you *are* leaving, and you won't take me? After everything, you'd just leave me here to rot while *you* get to run away? Coward!"

She turned away and strode down the street, but she only got a half-dozen steps when the dome over Ochana lit up. A man's face I didn't recognize, easily as large as several city blocks, peered down from the curved dome's inner surface. Lelah and I both stopped in our tracks to stare up at the placid face hovering over a business suit and tie.

The talking head spoke, and his voice seemed to come

from everywhere at once, at the same time both conversational in tone and loud enough to drown out every other sound. "Dragons of Ochana, this is an emergency broadcast. I don't have much time. They're coming for me already. King Rylan has been overthrown, the castle taken over by the Sepens family entourage in a surprise night-time raid. King Rylan's whereabouts are not currently known. As we know, he had no heir, and we can only presume King Rylan is dead. The laws of succession are clear. Rylan's brother abdicated his chance. Umbran Sepens sits on the Throne of Scales. Long live King Umbran and Crown Prince Trey, I guess. However they got there. Dragons of honor, you know your duty. Live up to it, no matter the cost."

As I stared in disbelief, a door opened behind the talking head and several armed and armored Wolands rushed into the room and grabbed the man, dragging him roughly from wherever he was recording. He offered no resistance, and they marched him out the door, letting it close behind them. For a couple of seconds, there was just the deathly still image of an empty, white studio, and then the signal flickered twice before vanishing altogether.

Lelah turned back towards me. “I’m going with you.” Her voice was strong with conviction, “and you can’t stop me.” She spat before stomping away into the night.

I stared up at that night sky for a long time without moving, feeling like I might throw up. I'd definitely made the right choice in leaving. My family was presumed dead. Eva and Cairo were no longer my friends. It was time for me to carve a new path. Start a new life. If nothing else, since becoming a Dragon, I've learned to follow the fates and the fates were pointing me towards Sanctuary.

CHAPTER 19

Mike led us in a downward spiral, broadcasting at all of us to keep our Mahier working double-time to keep us hidden as we traversed the coast west of Olympic National Park in Washington state. We flew low over a vast expanse of pine trees, heading west toward the setting sun. Soon after, the coastline loomed into view. To our right, a river wound back and forth before meeting the sea, and we seemed to travel more or less parallel to it.

That's the Quillayute River, Mike broadcast to us. *Sanctuary is on the coast, about a mile south of it. No real cities for miles, folks.*

We angled downward, heading toward a big village on the coast—larger than I'd expected. Behind it, there grew a big swath of old-growth red cedars, and I thought I even saw some real redwoods, though I was pretty sure redwoods weren't native to Washington. The cedars were just as big, though, and red, too. The effect was like a primordial redwood forest, older than civilization, surrounded by trees no more than a century old and mostly much younger. The shimmer of Mahier covered the old trees, showing where they'd been hidden from human eyes much like Paraiso was. Mike told us it would be hidden from humans but that we'd have no problem seeing it, and he'd been right.

We swooped in for a landing no more than a quarter mile outside of town. Pens full of livestock were scattered there, and we helped ourselves in Dragon form before summoning our human forms. Flying from Greenland non-stop had us all wiped out, but none of us had wanted to risk being tracked down by anyone pursuing us by our Mahier trail, so we'd put enough distance between us and Ochana that the trail would fade before they noticed we were gone. I'd learned of that talent among the Wolands during my time leading a wing. Ha. A lifetime ago...

When we finished devouring fresh meat, I noted two people standing off to the side, leaning against the pen's wooden fencing. Catching my eye, one waved and nodded in greeting. I walked over, reassured by warm smiles from a man and woman, both apparently in their mid-30s, whatever that was in Dragon years. Neither of them wore sashes, I observed immediately.

The woman said, "Hello, Dragons. I'm Mary, and this is Aiden. We've had a few more arrivals than normal lately, so we took the liberty of setting out some livestock so you could recharge. Tell me, what are you looking for out here, in the middle of nowhere?"

Mike stepped up beside me. "We seek Sanctuary, both me and my friends here."

The man she called Aiden grinned. "Welcome to Silver Cove, then. We grant you sanctuary. All are equal, or they start out so. What you make of yourself is up to you, not the color of your scales."

Nodding, Mary said, "Come, we'll show you around."

Lelah approached, looking more timid than usual. "Just like that? You don't want anything from us, first?"

Mary smiled. "No. New Dragons usually come with little to nothing. What could you give us but your labor? I think you've all likely had enough of being forced to give that. I know I had when I arrived. Feel free to ask your questions while we walk."

The town's edge was distinct, a curved line running north to south. There were no roads into town, and though there were narrow roads running perpendicularly throughout the side I could see, the only traffic was afoot or on bicycles. No cars or even quads or other motorized vehicles roamed these streets, giving it a peaceful air. People smiled and waved to each other—and none wore sashes.

The town was much larger than I'd expected, though. It was set up like a mandala, circles within circles that formed still more circles. Young trees grew along all the roads and between every building, thicker than the buildings themselves, giving an almost Paraiso-like illusion to the whole scene. The houses were far from the shanty shacks I'd envisioned, but instead were well-built structures ranging from cottage homes to low apartment buildings. Little parks dotted it every place circles came together within that mandala, too, but they looked more like gardens to me than parks.

Lelah let out a whistle. "Dang. This is not what I expected. I'm sorry," she added hastily at the end.

"I'm sure it's not. Look, Silver Cove is really a medium-sized coastal town. Most of our food comes from public gardens anyone can tend, if they ask for one, or from fishing. We're surrounded by heavy forests, but we have a community college, schools, and plenty of jobs. Even a lot of artisans, but there's some light manufacturing, packaging, services, and stores. Everyone gets basic housing. It will be just a room in a shared apartment to start, though many people find they enjoy the communal living and just never stop."

Aiden continued, "There are cottages, houses, and even a couple of ranches. It's a real town, but we're almost all Dragons. We all work together. That might take getting used to, I know, but you soon will wonder how you ever lived another way."

They spent that evening showing us the downtown area, the "main drag," where most of the shops were. Then, they showed our group to a vacant apartment, thankfully furnished, and let us collapse into an exhausted sleep. They left promising to come grab us pretty early in the morning for a more formal orientation, but I fell asleep the moment my head hit the pillow and didn't even remember Mary and Aiden leaving.

By my third day, I'd scrounged up a job working part-time in a fairly fancy restaurant called Flossy's that advertised a daily menu unique to whatever was in season or preservable. Its name was a play on words with the FLOSS style—farmed local, organic, seasonal, and sustainable. The owner was a funny red Dragon who'd put up his sword for a kitchen knife years earlier, and remembering my little taste-testing session back in Ochana's castle kitchen, I watched his every move. How he put strange foods together to create something delicious was a mystery, but he enjoyed my enthusiasm, I think, because by the end of that week, he'd gone ahead and removed my "probationary" status. Most jobs in town were part-time, so that wasn't a problem, and though it was fast, precise work, I found myself enjoying the job. That was a new experience, for me.

Lelah had never done anything but the typical labor of a Sien, so she found a job stocking shelves for several stores around town. She came back on our eighth day with brochures from the community college.

"Want to take a look at the classes they offer?"

I came out of the communal kitchen in our three-bedroom apartment carrying a meal I'd learned that day from Tedis, the chef and owner at Flossy's. "I'd forgotten there was a campus here. What are you thinking of taking?"

Lelah shrugged and smiled. "Well, definitely not manual labor. Actually, I was thinking of starting out with bookkeeping classes, then working up to an accounting associate degree. Sitting at a desk sounds really nice. What about you?"

"Nah." I couldn't help but return her infectious smile. "I enjoy what I'm doing. You should see the dishes my boss makes with just a handful of main ingredients, and we never know each day what we'll get at the market. It's controlled chaos, but I'd definitely rather swing a spatula than a sword."

She shrugged, looking at the brochures, then looked up at me. "Your boss, he's Tedis, right? Flossy's, I think."

"Yeah. Why?"

She held out one of her brochures. "He teaches the culinary arts classes at the community college. Maybe that's something you could take up."

"Maybe." I took the brochure and flipped through it. "The campus is having an Open House on Saturday. The restaurant is closed on weekends. I bet Tedis will be there. Are you going?"

She nodded. "Of course. I was hoping you'd come with me. A friendly face, and so forth. Will you?"

From the other end of the room, Mike said, "Go with her, Cole. I'll be off house-hunting anyway, so you'd just be stuck here alone and bored."

I looked back and forth, considering, but then I realized I was trying to make excuses where I had none. Besides, what could it hurt to just look?

The community college wasn't all that big, which wasn't surprising for a town that didn't technically exist. But it was accredited, ostensibly licensed as a distance-learning outreach campus, and the town itself paid for the licensing and its teachers' credentials. It was free to those who couldn't afford tuition, or almost free—I'd have to work one day each month, eight hours, to help keep the campus fit and clean. At least, that's what the brochures said. It was a cozy campus with small classes, its students split between those getting their general education credits out of the way for real college later, and those looking to pick up new trade skills or to refresh existing ones.

When we walked to the gates, it pretty much met the expectations the brochures had set. The tour guide was friendly enough, though he had the bored look of someone repeating the same thing for the fiftieth time. I wondered if he was doing his tuition-work day. At least he knew the answers to all the questions his little group posed. I'd already half decided some classes would at least be a good way to pass the time, especially with Mike looking for his own place. If I didn't like whatever roommate replaced him, it'd be good to have an excuse to get out of the apartment.

After lunch, we were free to roam around and go examine different classes. The professors came in for these Open House events every month or so, the guide had said, and I wanted to go see Tedis in a teacher's overcoat instead of a chef's cap, so I headed off alone to check it out.

I was halfway across the quad when I heard a woman say, "Cole? Is that you?"

The voice was so familiar, I found myself spinning around before I even realized it, and then I stared, slack-jawed. Arden? "You're really here? But, how?"

She grinned at me, clearly happy to see me. "After my father chased you off, I couldn't find you. I left home to keep searching since he had me basically locked up in the house, but after a week, I still couldn't find you. While he was busy throwing some stupid party, I gave up on finding you and took advantage of his distraction, and just followed an old blue Dragon out here."

"Wow. I helped put together the party if you can believe that. What I can't believe, though, is that I found you here, of all places."

"Actually, *I* found *you* here." She shrugged, pursing her lips, but then wrapped her arms around me and squeezed. When she stepped back, she was still grinning. "I got here yesterday morning, but when I heard about this event, I decided to check it out. Plus, they have dorm rooms here, and I'm not really liking my roommate. I got the impression she's used to having no roommates and would like to keep it that way, so..."

"Well, that just won't do, will it? Not at all. Can't have a Sepens daughter sharing a dorm room with commoners, not when she could have royalty for a roomie." I tried not to smile.

"Here, I'm not the daughter of Umbran Sepens, just another Dragon without a sash. But what are you talking about?"

"Oh, nothing. It's just that I have a three-bedroom apartment with the two people I came here with, and one of them is moving out, so there will be a vacant room. As I'm sure you can imagine, I'd rather have a roommate I know than some stranger moving in. What do you say, will you come live with me?" I tried to wink, but it felt like I just grimaces at her. "Just so I don't have to actually meet anyone new, of course."

Arden laughed at that, but then nodded. "I can think of worse roommates. Like the one I have now, for example. So, what classes are you going to take? I'm thinking of taking carpentry and furniture-making classes. Maybe I can apprentice with one of the artisans here. Half the town works for themselves like that, it seems."

I'd noticed the same thing, of course. "Oh yeah. This place breeds artisans like bacteria. But I'm working part-time at a fancy-pants restaurant, learning to cook. Funny thing, I found I really enjoy cooking, so I was thinking of taking culinary arts."

Arden rolled her eyes at me. "Yeah, right. You're a

prince. Shouldn't you be taking Machiavelli 101 or something?"

"Probably," I replied with a chuckle, but then I remembered I wasn't a prince anymore—everyone else had forgotten that, even more than I had. It was kind of appropriate, I supposed, given that I grew up thinking my parents were just normal, middle-class people. "But seriously, I'm just another Sien here. No one cares if you have silver scales, and you can be whatever you want to be in Silver Cove. I was really surprised to discover that I might want to be a chef, but it's true."

She put her hand on my arm, nodding. "It's great that you found something like a purpose, Cole. I'm sorry you had to come all the way out to Sanctuary to discover that. Maybe everyone seeing you as something you're not is turning out to be a blessing in disguise. The Prince of Ochana could never be a chef, you know. Too busy defending the world and training to lead the army someday."

Too true. I'd never have discovered how satisfying it is to cook for other people's enjoyment if not for Umbran's trickery.

Arden glanced at her phone, checking the time. "I have to go check out the class, but let's meet later, okay? I think you just cooked yourself up a new roommate. When can I meet your other one?"

"How about tonight over dinner? I'll cook," I replied without hesitating. I couldn't wait to introduce her to Lelah.

CHAPTER 20

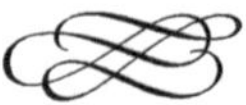

I set the Portobello mushrooms out on three plates, with parsley for garnish, along with lemon wedges. With a clean washcloth, I wiped the dribbled sautéing sauce off the plates. We were working on plating and presentation in my culinary arts classes, and of course, Lelah and Arden were my guinea pigs on most nights. It was a good thing they both chipped in for groceries, too—some of the food I was learning to make wasn't exactly cheap.

Once I had the plates set and garnish arranged, I picked up all three plates and headed out of the kitchen. The breakfast nook attached to the kitchen was the closest thing to a dining room we had in our apartment, but with only three of us, it was plenty big.

"Okay, let me know what you think of the presentation, okay? That's what I'll be graded on in our test on Friday. I had thought stuffed big ol' mushrooms would be easy to set out, but I forgot about the sauce."

Arden stared at the plates. "Mushrooms? That's it? I mean, they're big ones, but still."

I shrugged, wiping my hands, and then sat down as well. "Yeah. The sausage, you've had before and loved it. I used feta cheese and sun-dried tomatoes in the stuffing, with a creamy Parmesan polenta to balance out the tongue feel. We each got four of them, so it should be enough, but I guess if you're still hungry later, we can whip up something else."

Lelah took a bite and closed her eyes to savor the flavor, a good sign. "Delicious, Cole. Oh, I almost forgot to mention it, but some friends from work and I are going to sneak out into the redwoods tomorrow and stretch our wings. Get some flying in. I haven't summoned my Dragon since we got here. Want to come? You're both welcome to join me."

Arden scrunched up her face. "I know, right? I forgot I have a Dragon almost. I'm in. How often do we all have the same days off?"

She had me there. I hadn't stretched my wings since arrival, either. I said, "Definitely. I hope we don't get in trouble, but no one has told me I can't... I just don't see them flying around, so it might just be an unwritten rule."

"Well, until they write it down," Arden said, "I'll ask for forgiveness instead of permission."

Just like back in Ochana. "What time do we leave?"

When we arrived in the woods, Lelah's friends were already there with some of their other friends as well, and introductions between the ten of us took a minute. They all seemed like decent people, though, and Arden and I were openly welcomed. It was interesting how, in the absence of sashes to denote our color, everyone treated the others like *people,* not their color. Once again, I was glad I'd made the choice to come, even if I spent most of my free moments worrying about everyone we'd left behind in Ochana. There wasn't much I could do for them, though, and plenty to do in that forest.

Lelah, grinning, said, "Okay, on the count of ten, we all summon our Dragons. What do you say to a race? But you have to stay low. If you hit a tree, you're starting over. First one to make it one mile wins."

That sounded like a great idea, though it was hard to wait until she reached ten. Then, she called out the magic number, and we all shifted at once. Of course, everyone except for Arden saw me as a silver dragon, but it was okay. I wasn't the only Sien, and there were even two Wolands, but no one talked down to anyone else. It was nice. I fully expected a red Dragon to win the race, and I was right, though a blue Galian came in an awfully close second. On the race back, the other Woland won, but again, second place was no Woland. That time, Lelah took second.

One of her friends, Samantha, suggested team rabbit hunting. I hadn't hunted on the wing in quite a while, so that sounded like fun, and the others agreed. Of course, Lelah and Arden and I were on one team with two others. Everyone was talking at once, as excited as I was to indulge Dragon instincts again.

"So, should we split up and cover more ground that way?" Arden asked.

"Actually," I said, as an idea dawned on me, "I have a plan. Something we used to do... Something I saw before. When Woland wings in Ochana train together, they used to have a 'rabbit rally,' where they'd get into a formation like a big 'V' and spiral over a forest, working their way in from outside in. If they spotted a target, the outside Dragon dove for it, then got back into formation on the innermost position. The rabbits they didn't see spooked and bolted toward the center. At the end, when the spiral got tight, there'd be too many rabbits to catch, even, all scurrying around. Want to try it?"

Lelah grinned. "That sounds like fun. It's what the soldiers did to train?"

I nodded. "Oh, yeah. Worked great, too. Lelah, why don't you take the lead, and the rest of us can form up behind you. Everyone just stays about ten yards back and to one side of whoever is before them. When we get to the rabbit rally, in the middle, whoever's on center calls out to engage, and everyone dives together, so the rabbits don't have time to scurry away before we get as many talons down at once as possible."

John, a friend of Samantha's on our team, grinned. "Oh

yeah, that sounds awesome. We'll twist their tails in this hunt, by Aprella."

At first, of course, no one knew where they should be and seemed to forget which wing was their left and which one was their right, but I had enough experience leading a wing to gently nudge them into formation with directed thoughts. Doing that and staying in formation myself kept me too busy to look for rabbits, but we had the rest for that, and anyway, the big rally would be at the end. And by then, I'd finally gotten them used to staying in formation. When I at last got a moment to channel some Mahier into my Dragonsight, zooming in ahead of us, I gasped, smoke billowing from my snout. So many rabbits! And deer, too, but it was the rabbits we were after. It looked like a carpet of bunnies, down there.

Arden happened to be at the tip of the reversed V, and broadcast, "Ready? *Engage!*" Her excitement rang clear even through her thought-speak, and it was contagious.

My heart soared higher than my Dragon, and as one, we dove, strafing the rabbit rally—I got three on that first pass alone. We made three more passes, and in the end, I had a brace of ten bunnies. Lelah and Arden, more agile than I, caught even more. Between the five of us, we had sixty of them or so.

The other team returned, grinning until they saw our haul. They had maybe twenty, altogether.

Samantha, on the other team, was awestruck, grinning as she congratulated us, and I don't think I ever saw Lelah look prouder. That would have made me smile too if I hadn't already been grinning wide enough to bare every fang in my snout.

Of course, none of it went to waste. We pooled the rabbits and split them evenly, with Lelah getting the extra two as the winning team leader, and devoured them in seconds. It was a fantastic time, and nothing tastes as great as fresh, wild rabbits. Only once we'd finished did we summon our humans again.

That was when I spotted two big, red Dragons flying toward us, low over the forest. Some of the others turned to see what I was staring at, and the celebrating ended rather promptly.

"I hope we're not in trouble," Lelah said, mirroring my own thoughts.

The two Wolands descended, summoning their human forms as they touched down smoothly. Approaching the group, it was hard to read their expressions, and I braced myself to ask for forgiveness, since we'd neglected to ask for permission.

One of them said, "Good afternoon, people. We've been watching you all doing your thing out here, and to be honest, I'm curious. Who taught you guys to fly like that?"

He was looking at our two Wolands, but they both shrugged.

I said, "I hope I didn't do anything wrong. We were just having some fun on our day off."

The new Woland who'd spoken previously said, "No

trouble. Where'd you learn to fly like that?"

I was nervous, and before I'd even thought it through, I heard myself say, "Jericho taught me. Did I do it wrong?"

He cocked his head, eying me head to toe, then shrugged. "Interesting. You did it as well as any wingleader. Do you think you could train other non-Wolands to do that? Do you know more maneuvers?"

I nodded. "I guess I could. Sure, I know all the formations."

The second Woland finally smiled, nodding. "Excellent. I'm Jonathan Maxwell, Silver Cove's mayor, and I think you just found yourself a full-time job, young man. You okay with that? Of course, it means you'll get to fly all day—"

"Yes!" I couldn't believe my luck. "Of course," I added with a bit more dignity. "I'd be delighted to train whoever wants to learn. Even if I have to fly every single day."

Jonathan Maxwell had me start the very next day, cutting short my time off, but I didn't even mind. As we biked home that evening, my thoughts were a jumble of nerves as I considered how to train even more Dragons, but I knew I could do it. We'd had no Wolands on our team, and we'd won—they didn't need red scales to learn to fly like Wolands.

Over the next few days, I started out easy, just flying in basic formations. For the most part, the Dragons were happy just to have overt permission to fly around, but they also seemed interested in the training itself. It was novel for them, and that made it easy for me, really. On the first day, Arden had given me the bright idea of using the human version of DragonTools to keep track of who had attended which training sessions, and Lelah suggested making each session into some kind of game. They responded well and with enthusiasm.

But when we moved from basic formations into actual maneuvers, attendance swelled. Search and Evasion, or SeAV, was particularly popular, with everyone competing to see how long they could go before the "patrol" caught the "intruder." Lelah, surprisingly, was particularly good at that, and took the top spot. She was small and sneaky, and her agility made her maneuvers look like gymnastics, almost ballet-like. And when she was on the search team, she was wickedly effective—no one got away from her for long.

Arden, however, didn't participate other than helping with some of the administration stuff. It was all voluntary, though, and I was glad for the help, so I didn't pressure her. But one day, as the last morning SeAV run was drawing to a close with Lelah finally being cornered and submitting, I turned to Arden and, out of curiosity, asked, "Why don't you join them? You're pretty agile, and you'd do well with this stuff. Plus, it's fun."

She looked up from the tablet on which she was typing notes and frowned. "I don't want to."

"I know. I love having the help with all the records, mind

you. I appreciate what you're doing. I'm just curious as to why, that's all."

She shrugged. "It makes me nervous. I guess it's hard to overcome the stupidity we're taught by our parents. Or something. Whatever the reason, I just get sweaty palms thinking about it. I'm happy just helping out with the logistics of it all. That okay?"

"Of course." I smiled, mostly for her benefit. I'd seen her fly, competed with her in play, and I knew what she could do. It was a shame, but I wasn't going to pressure her to do something she didn't want to do, so I just said, "Heck, if it weren't for your help, all these records would be a mess—if they even got done at all. You are helping, just in a different way. Thanks for that."

Her eyes locked onto something over my shoulder. I turned and saw the first Dragons returning from the last exercise. I started to raise my hand to wave when I saw something else. Some*one* else. A figure at the edge of the woods, and then more figures. They stepped out from underneath the forest cover, and there was another, and then another.

It was an Elf. *Elves,* I corrected myself. And behind them, there were Trolls. They were smiling, and one made her way toward me. I was dumbfounded. There were too many for it to be a scout team. No, I realized, *there were Elves and Trolls living in the redwoods*.

I drew myself up and marched forward to greet the neighbors we never knew we had.

CHAPTER 21

Several days later, I took a break from classes, both the ones I taught and the ones in which I studied. A new orientation had come around, and I'd volunteered to help. The first thing I noticed was that the crowd was smaller than before and consisted this time entirely of Siens and Galians.

The second thing I noticed was that they were far thinner than I had been when I arrived, and they had sunken, baggy eyes. They looked exhausted. As someone gave the welcome speech I'd heard only recently myself, I nudged in among the other Siens and listened to their quiet conversations. Most had downcast eyes, not looking up at the speaker. From the snippets I overheard, it was clear things had gone downhill in Ochana, and I'd escaped just in time.

My curiosity got the better of me. I asked a Sien standing beside me, "What's going on in Ochana? I left without too much hassle."

She didn't look up at me. "Things are worse every day. We're guarded to keep us from leaving, given no choice in jobs anymore. Those who resist find it is harder to work for food in chains."

"Aprella's ghost," I spat. "Working for food? Has anyone told this to Jericho?"

The Sien finally looked up, and I swore she looked sadly at me. "No. Siens and Galians aren't allowed to speak except to our own kind, unless it's to take orders. But do you think he doesn't know?"

"Not allowed to?" I felt smoke curling up around my nose, rising from my nostrils. "We don't need permission to speak. We're free Dragons, working for the greater good. We—"

"You dream, Dragon. It's impossible even to pretend anymore, not when any green or red Dragon can beat you for speaking out of turn. Not when we have to work willingly if we don't want to work in chains." She shook her head and then turned back toward the welcome speaker, going silent and ignoring my efforts to get her to keep talking.

My ire rose, but not at her. Well, with so few new arrivals, Silver Cove didn't need my help at this orientation. I made my way back through the thin crowd behind me and headed for home. I had to do something else. Anything else.

I made it in record time.

Stepping inside, I found Arden sitting on the living room couch.

"Hey, Cole. You're home early, aren't you?" She set down the book she'd been reading, looked at me again, and froze. "What's wrong?"

"You should have seen the new Dragons, Arden. They're dirty, skinny, and broken." I paced the narrow open area in the living room, turning sharply left with almost every step, but I hardly noticed I was doing it. "I've got to get out. Come with me? I need someone to talk to."

She slid her book off her lap, carefully placing a bookmark within it before setting it on the couch cushion. "Sure, Cole. If you need to talk and walk, we can do that."

I grabbed a hoodie—the weather in Washington was unpredictable at best, especially along the coast—and held out her jacket as I reached for the door. I don't think I said a word as we walked aimlessly, ending up at the little town's outskirts where the redwoods began in earnest.

Arden looked around, then leveled her gaze at me. "Okay, Cole, spill it. What's eating at you?"

I glared, not so much at her, but through her. "You should have seen them. You should see what your father is doing to them."

She flinched as though I'd struck her.

I continued, "The new arrivals—there were half as many as when we went through our orientation, Arden. The ones who did make it are scrawny and tired. Like, *really* skinny.

None of them will look you in the eyes when you talk to them, and I overheard them whispering about how they aren't *allowed* to talk to anyone but their own kind unless a Woland or Leslo deigns to speak to them first. Umbran is forcing them to work. I don't mean pressuring them to meekly accept their lot in life, either. He's putting them in chains if they don't work hard enough. Chains, Arden!"

She set her hand on my shoulder lightly, then lifted it away like she was afraid to touch me. I didn't mean to make her flinch from me, but Aprella knew, I was seriously angry.

"I thought it was bad when I was there. Your father has set up work gangs, honest to goodness chain gangs of workers. They aren't even pretending that we're all different-but-equal anymore."

"Oh my go... By Aprella, I mean. How could that happen? Why isn't someone doing something about it?"

"And just how should I know? He's *your* father." I instantly regretted snapping at her when she flinched away from me again, but that did nothing to calm me down. "We've got to fix this. You and me. I'm the Keeper, even if no one even knows it anymore, and you're his daughter."

She glared at me, but her tone was even as she replied, "That's right. I'm his daughter, I'm not him. I didn't do this, and neither did you."

"I sure did. The minute I ran away from my duty, I let this happen. I should have known I couldn't run from my problems."

"Okay, Cole. I hear you. What do you mean to do?"

That was the rub. I had no idea what to do. "We owe it to them to... To do something. Anything! I've got to go back. I'll try anything, but we've got to help them. I was hoping you'd have an idea."

"Cole." She peered into my eyes, her hard expression softening. "We can't save everyone from themselves, you know. Sometimes bad things happen, even to good people. Especially to them."

"Them? You can still say that? Those are *our* people being chained up and starved, don't you get it? There's got to be something we can do to fix it. I saved the damned world; surely, I can save a few Dragons. Right? Come with me, please."

She watched me for a long moment, seconds ticking by, then pursed her lips before saying, "And do what?"

"I don't know. That's why we're talking. Ochana needs us right now, and I can no longer hide here in this sanctuary and pretend, not anymore."

"You know I can't go back there," she whispered. I had to strain to hear her words. "I was a prisoner to Umbran long before anyone got shackled. It's why I'm here. We can't save them, Cole. We're just two Dragons, and you aren't even the Keeper. Not anymore."

I was about to snarl something I was certain I would regret when a shadow detached itself from one of the redwoods. A person-sized shadow with pointy ears. Arden and I both jerked in surprise as an Elf woman seemed to step into our world from some shadowy dimension. In a far cry from the smiles the Elves had worn at our earlier meeting, this one glared openly at us.

"Dragons," the Elf hissed. "You dare come here, after what your people are doing to us?"

"What are you talking about, you silly little Elf?" I instantly regretted my words, but they were out, and I couldn't take them back. "We're not doing anything to you."

Arden nodded. "I'm afraid we don't know what you're talking about. Surely you heard some of our conversation. We're from Silver Cove, and as far as I know, we haven't done anything to you."

"Or to us?" Another voice rang out, this one deeper, more guttural. A shadow seemed to crawl up from beneath a redwood's massive rootstocks and step into the waning sunlight.

"Trolls, too? What kind of monsters do you think Silver Cove people are?" Arden's eyes went wide as she realized what she had said, and I eyed the newcomers both, trying to gauge their responses.

Silence hung in the air as seconds ticked by.

At last, the Elf said, "That's a very good question. Why are you letting your people attack us?"

"What do you mean? We're not attacking anyone."

"Well, Dragons are," the troll said, practically spitting the word like it was venomous.

The Elf nodded. "Your people are attacking Elf and Troll villages all over the globe, but you claim to know nothing?"

A multi-colored hue illuminated everything I saw, and

my eyes itched. I realized they were glowing, and smoke from my nose irritated them. I took a few deep breaths and tried to calm myself. Instead of answering the Elf, I looked Arden in the eyes. "How can Umbran be doing this, Arden? Attacking Elves and Trolls now, too?"

The Elf put her fists on her hips and shifted until she faced me head-on. "But you're the *Keeper*. Surely *you* know what's going on if anyone does."

Arden stared at the Elf openly. "Say that again?"

The Elf rubbed one elbow with her other hand, but her gaze stayed fixed on me. "Well, you are, right? You're a Keeper of Dragons, and since there are only two, and you're male, that makes you Colton, son of King Rylan. Our hide-away village has been attacked, and wow, what a coincidence, the Dragon king's son is wandering around the same enchanted forest."

"Yeah, but..." My voice trailed off.

Arden finished my sentence. "But how did you recognize the Keeper?"

The woman laughed aloud. "Really? Is there anyone among the Races of Truth who doesn't yet know about you? Colton, half of the Keeper of Dragons and heir to the throne of Ochana."

The Troll sniffled and wiped his nose with his sleeve. "Not me. Dragons... Humans... they all look the same. But his aura... Aha! Now that *was* described to me, and it's distinct."

The Elf woman smiled wanly at her Troll associate. "Yes,

I see a sort of 'halo' around you, Keeper. I might never remember what makes your ridiculous nose look different from any other Dragon's, but I'll never forget your halo. Nonetheless, Colton, someone has been attacking Elven villages, both hidden enclaves like the one here and official ones around North America. Your 'halo' tells me you're being honest, though. You aren't the one attacking us. Nonetheless, someone is. You seemed sure it was your friend's father. Is that right?"

"I'm fairly certain he both knows about the attacks and has done nothing at all to halt them. My friend here is Arden, and you have my word that I am convinced she had nothing to do with them. She's in Silver Cove in large part to get away from messy family entanglements with her father."

The woman sucked on her teeth and nodded at us both. "Fine. I believe you, Keeper. I'd be grateful if you could ask whoever is in charge of Silver Cove, though. Maybe they've heard rumors about who is ultimately responsible for these recent attacks."

I agreed—it was the least I could do, and frankly, I felt a surprising amount of gratitude toward her just for recognizing me. Going and talking to the mayor was the least I could do for her.

Mayor Johnathan Maxwell didn't hesitate to let me into his office. Of course, he asked how the training and fitness programs were coming, and I answered truthfully that the townsfolk were catching on faster than I could come up with lessons. But when I followed that up with questions of my own, about attacks on Elven villages, he looked sad, and his cheeks puffed out as he blew out a harsh breath.

"Sorry, I don't know anything about any attacks on Elven settlements, and the only such settlement I even know of is Paraiso, and that's by reputation only. You said the Elf knew you by reputation, as well, just from a whiff of your aura?"

"Yeah."

"And everyone else you've met doesn't remember you exist, at least, not as the Crown Prince of King Rylan or Keeper of Dragons, right?"

I nodded. "Heck, do you?" I already knew the answer to that question.

Johnathan frowned, his head shaking faintly. "Sorry. I can't say I do. But... Everyone's energy is a bit like a halo, you know. When I look at you, I can almost see yours, like a holograph that looks familiar but that I can't quite place. I can't recall where I'd seen it before."

Well, the Elves could. Although I'd gone out of my way to avoid thinking about my old life, that was easier said than done, but with at least one Elf remembering who I was, I felt a small, faint ember of hope inside. I knew it was pointless to get optimistic about something that changed nothing, but Arden's words from back on Ochana came back to me then, unbidden—*"It'll all get better, in the end,*" she'd once said a vision told her. A vision of Eva, possibly.

The sudden thought of her name struck me like a hammer to the chest. I had avoided thinking of Eva as best I could, but memories didn't like to be long denied. The memory of my fellow Keeper basically turning her back on me as easily as if I'd been a stranger… Well, that memory wouldn't leave me alone, either.

I left with no more information than I had when I arrived, but a lot more burdens on my mind.

CHAPTER 22

The following Monday, I decided to change things up a bit for the Dragonflight classes I taught. Instead of competitive races, challenges, or maneuvers, we would play games and communally score our best aerial athletes' music-based performance as they went through a crude obstacle course we had set up previously. I was surprised at the enthusiastic response from the day's class, though I'd known it would be popular. I just hadn't thought it would be *that* popular. No, that wasn't quite true. Everyone had been fairly down in the dumps since the refugees seeking Sanctuary had begun to arrive looking so skinny and often wounded. This bit of positivity was a much-needed respite from all that, not to mention from my own pains and worries.

The morning went by in a quiet camaraderie with

Dragons of every color, mostly watching our top talents blaze artful, athletic trails through the obstacle course. The O-course was a mix of ground, air, and shifting stations meant more to develop agility and body awareness than actual fitness—with Mahier to fuel them, Dragons didn't really have to worry about fitness, especially not when they'd summoned their Dragon forms. We'd already set up bleachers along one of the O-course edges, and they were far more packed with watching Dragons than most days.

Although Arden would have been great at the O-course challenge, she continued to refuse to participate. Lelah, however, had no such qualms. She was fast, lithe, and sneaky! But although she dominated most others in terms of the time it took her to get through it and the elegance with which she completed the individual challenges, she was no gymnast or dancer, and she seemed pretty well aware of that fact. She only gave her performances the most basic of artistic flair, and that cost her in points. Basically, it was still neck-and-neck between her and three others to see who would take the highly coveted, non-existent, hypothetical trophy.

A ripple passed through the assembled audience. I squinted to see what was going on, but to my surprise, I discovered they weren't looking at the contestants, but over their shoulders and up into the sky. Reflexively, I followed their pointing and staring. I cupped a hand over my eyes, forgetting for a moment that I could just use Mahier to magically enhance my eyesight, even in my human form.

When I did finally remember, I telescoped in on two dots in the distant sky, and my breath instantly caught in my chest. Those were two Dragons, and two I knew very well indeed. Or rather, I once had. But they were flying too slowly, their wings hardly flapping.

I stepped off the bleachers and summoned my Dragon as my feet met only air. It was hard getting airborne and getting some momentum, but surging some Mahier under my wings took care of that, and soon I was close enough to focus on private communications.

Welcome to Silver Cove. How badly are you two wounded?

I'm somewhat injured, just a bothersome flesh wound. My name is Cairo, and this is my partner, Eva. I'm her Vera Salit, *the first bona fide soulmates documented among our kind in centuries, I'm told.*

Without thinking, I immediately began to look her over for wounds of her own.

Cairo said, *She's not wounded, not physically.* His voice in my head sounded weary and tense. I could feel his overpowering concern for her, though. His worries shook his thoughts, dulling their edges. *She is ill, in spite of Elf and Dragon magic alike. Yesterday, we decided to leave Paraiso, for her own health and wellbeing.*

Eva's thought-speech interrupted him. *I may not be injured, but Cairo is. It isn't a mortal wound, but there is so much going on in Ochana that finding an available Galian healer proved impossible.*

Even for the Keeper of Dragons, Cairo added.

She nodded. *So it seems. We did go first to Ochana, seeking aid from King Rylan, but…*

Cairo shrugged. *He was in no position to help us.*

I wondered why he was hedging his words but let him continue uninterrupted.

But Eva needs help, and I would not refuse a healer's service, if only to get this one to shut up about my little scratch. So, we came out here. I think we used to have some kind of property off the Puget Sound, but I can't be certain.

The memory is hazy for me, too, Eva added.

I reversed direction with mid-air gymnastics, then glided up to match Eva's course and heading, Cairo on her other side. *Why here? Why not somewhere else farther from royal court politics?*

Cairo's eyes crinkled at the corners as he laughed for a moment. *In part, it's because the Keeper and I both remember… well…*

Eva's wingtip fingers and the talons in which they ended twitched a few times, a startling admission of irritation for any Dragon, but for stoic Eva, she might as well have written her frustration in neon ink on a day-glow billboard. I'd known her almost our entire lifetimes. But when she replied, her thought-speech revealed none of that.

The truth is, he and I both think we remember another Keeper of Dragons. That's crazy, I know, but it's true. We just cannot recall any details of such a person, if they indeed exist.

Cairo tipped his wings, nodding. *Yes, we hoped to find some clue in Sanctuary that might tell us whether we just shared a dream through our Soulmate bond, or if there was indeed some kind of miraculous second Keeper. Hilarious, I know. But where better to start looking, when the official records don't coincide with memories and a few well-placed bruises make flying difficult?*

Eva said, *we only just learned of this place. King Gaber of the Elves said that he, too, now had some fleeting memory of a second Keeper, and that we might find a hiding Dragon here, as well as rest and healing for ourselves.*

I'd known Eva for twenty years, even if she didn't even know who I was anymore. I could tell without looking that she was hiding something. What if they were deluded into believing Sanctuary was a threat to Ochana? A Keeper on a mission could be the last thing Silver Cove needed to meet, depending on the mission. There were powerful forces in Ochana, such as the Sepens family, who would love to have an outside enemy to point at. Sanctuary would be little more than a speed bump to Ochana's army, but he was not above using them as a nebulous enemy to solidify his position.

My head started to spin at the paranoid thoughts running through it. It was time to go fishing for information. Somewhat disingenuously, I broadcast directly to them both, *so what on Earth could possibly keep King Rylan from helping the Keeper of Dragons and her* Vera Salit *when they needed it?*

Cairo's reply came immediately. *We need to talk to whoever is in charge in Sanctuary, actually. And probably everyone living there right after that, but we'll leave that decision up to your king or whoever.*

Eva's tone was less brusque when she added, *please don't*

take offense, but we don't know you well enough to tell you *before we tell the people in charge. I have no doubt they'll want everyone to know what we told them, though. Patience, young Sien.* She chuckled, making the fire in her gullet boil and bubble. To a Dragon, that sound was almost cute, like a cat's purring.

I slammed down my mental shields hard and fast. In no way did I want them to even sense the flavor of the thoughts her reply had sent streaking through me. First, a quiet rage washed through me, and the world took on a multi-hued glimmer as my eyes flared with light. I could hide the thoughts, but not that.

But I wasn't really angry. I was hurt, I realized. She'd known me almost her entire life, and yet neither of them cared enough to remember me. All the pain and terror we'd suffered together to fight the dark Elf menace, ending the Time of Fear… That all meant nothing to her or Cairo. Less than nothing. I wasn't her only true friend for her entire life. No, I was just some random Sien being too nosy.

I flapped my wings as I angled downward, the better to pick up speed. I snarled, my thoughts safe within a thick magical shield of pure Mahier. The sooner I dumped them off with the mayor and got on with my life, the better. And good riddance to fake friends.

As politely as I could manage, I led Eva and Cairo into the mayor's office and gave his assistant the quick version of everything I knew. It wasn't much, but it got his full attention. That done, I headed for the door, throwing a lazy wave and head-nod at the two people I'd thought were my best friends.

"Johnathan Maxwell is the mayor's name. I'm sure he'll see you shortly. Good luck."

Cairo grunted. Eva feigned a smile—as if I didn't know her well enough to tell immediately. Ha. I couldn't get out of that office fast enough.

I was halfway to the door to get the heck out of there when Johnathan called out my name. "Cole, don't leave, yet. You can't just dump two strange Dragons in my office without introducing me."

I turned around and found him smiling at me. I forced myself to relax, or to try to look relaxed at least, and suddenly felt... foolish? Selfish? I wasn't sure what would be the right word under the circumstances, but there definitely was one that fit, and it wasn't one I would have been proud to wear.

Worse, the mayor was right. I'd let my own wounded feelings get in the way of something that seemed likely to be awfully important to every free Dragon in Silver Cove.

I tried to fill my head with excuses, hoping it would leave no room in my troubled thoughts for doubt and embarrassment. That didn't work out very well, though. I took a deep breath, and marched back toward him.

"Cairo, Eva, let me introduce the honorable Johnathan Maxwell, closest thing Silver Cove has to a ruler and a darn fine person who has helped hundreds of Dragons over the years. Mayor Maxwell, this is Eva, Keeper of Dragons, and her Woland protector, Cairo. He also happens to be her *Vera Salit*."

Johnathan's eyes widened and clicked over to them. "The Keeper of Dragons? Here, in Silver Cove? And I was under the impression that the idea of *Vera Salit* was just an overblown fairytale. Is this true, he's really your soulmate?"

Eva smiled as she looked at Cairo and said, "Yes, it is. It's hard to explain, but I can feel our Mahier swirling and blending when we're near each other, and I feel mine reaching out to his when we're apart." Then, her smile faded. "I am sorry to say, that's not why we're here, though."

She paused, and as I watched her, I noticed her whole balance shifting forward and back, ever so slightly, and her right knee intermittently shaking. That's when I noticed she was a lot paler than I remembered her. I'd been too wrapped up in my own feelings to notice earlier. Perhaps that was from staying mostly under a jungle canopy for so long now, but I doubted it. I was watching her illness at work in her body, whatever it was.

My hurt feelings seemed to melt away. I was still angry that she didn't remember me, but the rage was now directed at the universe, not at her. The realization made me look Cairo over more carefully, as well. They'd said he was hurt... Sure enough, I found a spot on his waist, about the size of a large handprint, where his red uniform shirt was darker than the rest of it. Blood.

I heard myself saying, "Mayor, they both need healers. Our best healers. She's the Keeper of Dragons, but something is wrong, and Cairo is doing his best not to bleed on the rug right now."

"Cole, I don't— "

"Sir, they tried to treat her in Paraiso, and they both tried Ochana, but here they are. I mean, the Keepers did save the world, including this little part of it. I'm not trying to tell you what to do, and I hope you don't take it that way, but we've got to do something for them. Right?"

Surprisingly, I didn't really care what way he took it, so long as Eva and Cairo were healed.

The mayor cocked his head at me for half a second, then clicked his teeth with his tongue, making a *tsk* sound. After a moment's hesitation, he said, "Well, of course we must, Cole. This is the Keeper of Dragons, after all, and if half the old legends about soulmates are true, if we lose him, we'd lose her shortly after. They are each other's strength—and each other's weakne— "

He paused, mid-word. His eyebrows furrowed, and his eyes became unfocused for a second. Eva and Cairo glanced at one another. I couldn't really blame them, because I thought it was pretty odd, too. When his eyes lost their glazed look a couple seconds later, he said, "Am I crazy? Weren't there two Keepers, once?"

Eva's eyes went wide. "You, too? We had the same thought, but neither of us was certain we weren't just half remembering one of our dreams. Cairo and I do that a lot, so it can be hard to tell. We went to Ochana to look, but... Actually, that's what led to our coming here. In part, it is because we do need some help, ourselves. But also, in part, we're looking for someone. If there's another Keeper of Dragons and they aren't in Ochana, I'd think they had to be blending in here, in Sanctuary. Wouldn't you think?"

Cairo grunted. "Going to Ochana is the reason I could use some help in the first place. Also, it's why we came to see you. We have news that may not be very welcome, but ignorance isn't bliss, in this case."

Mayor Maxwell took a deep breath. Held it. Let it out slowly. "So, it's bad news, then. Okay, hit me with it. Better to know than to hope it goes away."

Cairo smiled briefly. "Good to hear. I can appreciate that. It's pragmatism. Eva, will you tell them? It's... kind of painful for me."

The room looked like it began to slowly swim in a circle, the walls bending inward slightly, making the room smaller. So, it really was bad news, then. I tried to quiet my heart pounding in my ears so I could hear what they said over the thud, thud, thud noise.

Eva looked up at the ceiling as she nodded. "I understand. Well, the reason we couldn't get a healer to look at me in Ochana and the reason Cairo now needs a healer as well are one and the same. King Rylan has been essentially deposed—"

I found myself physically taking a step away from her, as though distance would change her words...

"... And Umbran Sepens has taken over the entire disc. He rules it with an iron fist forged of Woland soldiers."

The mayor toppled back into his chair, his knees buckling. "But how? They took oaths! They're soldiers. Rylan's soldiers."

His words were echoes of my thoughts when I had seen that newscaster in Ochana... a fact I was to scared to say out loud. My cheeks flushed warm, realizing I'd been too wrapped up in my own trash to notify even the mayor.

Cairo grimaced. "Not all of them are traitors. Not yet. A core of them have always placed their first loyalty to the noble house that sponsors their unit, and to Ochana second. Most of the noble houses have always railed against the end of the old ways, glorifying and exaggerating it far beyond any caste system we ever had in reality. Sepens tapped into their elitist hearts and their sense of losing power since Rylan's father first forced 'this whole equality nonsense' on them, ignoring their demands—and winning, politically."

This was unbelievable. "I can't believe you, Cairo. You look up to that train wreck of a king? The whole reason Eldrick and his dark Elves almost won their war against the whole world was Rylan's father ignoring his oaths and duties to the world." Johnathan, nodding, stood back up, leaning his hands on his desk for support. "And he ignored both duty and tradition when he abandoned the Races of Truth, shattering alliances that had lasted a thousand years."

Well, he wasn't wrong. I jumped back in. "We barely rebuilt those alliances in the *Crowns* Accord in time to stop

Eldrick at all. Where were these so-called nobles then, huh? Where was this love for 'tradition' when the last king was abandoning our allies and duty?"

Cairo let out a long breath. "Look, I didn't do it, so maybe go yell at Rylan's father. I'm bleeding all over the rug because of Umbran, so don't lump me in with him. Got it? Truth is, the people who support him now didn't scream about what the former king did because it meant they didn't have to go help a bunch of ground-dwellers who were literally beneath them. King Rylan's building the Crowns Accord, with all those lesser races being our equals, well... That didn't taste as smooth and creamy to them, okay?"

Eva held up her hands between the two of us. "Enough. And for the record, Umbran has the king locked up in his own castle. There are lots of Wolands loyal to Rylan, or who don't like what's going on with Umbran in charge, but with their liege a hostage, what would you have them do? Most of them fought alongside the Elves only a short time ago, remember. You think they want to raid all those villages to steal magical items Dragons can't even use? No. You think they like watching the worst ones oppressing the same Dragons they swore to protect with their lives? No."

As she spoke, her voice grew louder, higher pitched. Her cheeks had turned bright pink by the time I held up my hands, surrendering. She had a point.

While she took quick, deep breaths and counted to ten, I began to pull in Tillium. The Elves' magic literally hung in the air, waiting to be absorbed, once I opened myself to drawing it in. It took only seconds to gather enough for my purpose. Then, I quieted my mind, imagining a blank piece of paper. Slowly, over that blank paper envisioned only in my own mind, I formed a face. Ears. Hair. A familiar set of features that belonged to an Elven woman I hadn't even known lived among the same trees we did until a short time ago.

In moments, focusing with the enhanced energy of Tillium so abundantly around me, I felt something like a *click,* inside my mind, and in that moment, I was no longer alone in my own thoughts. *Greetings, Keeper Colton,* the Elf thought with me. No, *to* me...

Greetings, I replied inside my head. *Two things. First, I could use your help in healing both the Dragons you found me with earlier.*

And second?

I smiled, or maybe only thought I had. *Second, I know who has attacked your village, and it's not just here. It's everywhere. And I know what they want. I'll tell you whether you help my friends or not, but I hope you will.*

The connection abruptly cut off, but it was okay. My last fleeting glimpse of our shared thoughts told me all I needed to know to put my worries about Eva and Cairo to rest.

CHAPTER 23

I rose in the morning and showered, but instead of putting on something warm to fight off the slightly chilly air in the damp, shadowy forest undergrowth, I put on a pair of black slacks and shoes that shined like a mirror, and a white button-up, long-sleeve shirt. I hadn't put on a tie in quite some time, so getting the darn thing to hang at the right length and angle was highly tedious—and yet, I could hardly stand still long enough to get it on. The moment it looked properly tied, I bounded for the door, snatching my black coat from the rack on my way out. I didn't even bother to put it on before I left, just wrestled my way into it along the way. I double-checked the giant buttons down its front before I got to my destination.

I paused, grinning, long enough to take a deep breath, then strode in through the back door. It took a second to adjust to the bright light reflecting off the white tile floor, walls, and counters. At a long island in the center, two sous chefs in black jackets only a bit more ornate than mine stood chopping vegetables, flanking a familiar, grinning man in the pristine white coat everyone suspected he slept in, he wore it so much.

When Tedis saw me, his grin broadened, and he called my name as I approached him. "Colton! Welcome back, young man. We've missed you these past couple of weeks, both in class and in my kitchen. How's training?"

"That part's going well, Chef. Thanks. I've missed working, and the classes, too. I happen to have a couple days off from teaching Dragons how to fly, so I was hoping you could find something useful for me to do around here, sir."

Tedis shrugged. "Maybe I could let you waste some time pretending to be useful, sure. Do you remember how to cut potatoes or carrots allumette?"

I paused dramatically, then nodded. Hesitantly, I asked, "Quarter-inch square by two or three inches long?"

He rolled his eyes, knowing very well I wasn't uncertain of it.

I asked, "Potatoes or carrots today, Chef? Will forty pounds be enough?"

I can only describe the expression he wore as bemused when he replied. "Carrots, please. And almost certainly more than enough unless you're truly terrible at cutting them."

I nodded and grabbed two huge sacks of carrots, then

wandered over to an open space at the island with everyone else. "I'll try not to waste more than thirty pounds, then."

He paused from his chopping to look at me across the island. "Thanks for coming in, by the way. We've been hammered with customers the last few days. Still, you didn't have to wander here in uniform on your first day off in two weeks."

"It's no problem. I missed working in here with you and your team. Let me know if you need anything else." I set the carrots on one end of the counter, which faced the open restaurant area, and started cutting the carrots allumette style. After a few minutes, I found my rhythm again, and I soon had a mountain of cut carrots. I was setting those neatly onto a serving tray when the door opened. I looked up and paused as my eyes found the familiar face of Cairo.

He crossed the floor but stopped halfway across and stared at me. It was hard to work with Cairo staring at me, especially when I wanted nothing more than to grab his shirt and shake him, demanding to know why one of my best friends didn't even know who I was. I envisioned throttling Umbran. He had taken more than my identity from me—he took my oldest friends.

Finally, I set the kitchen knife down, wiped my hands, and went out to the restaurant floor to approach him. "What do you want, Cairo? I'm working."

"I see that." He pursed his lips. "I keep thinking about what you said. But I feel like there's something different about you today, standing here. Different? No... Almost familiar. Like I know you."

I wanted to scream that he did know me. It took a moment to get that under control. With a sigh, I turned around and headed back to the kitchen. "Take care of Eva," I said over my shoulder as I crossed the kitchen threshold, then got back to work cutting another mountain of carrots, this time with my back to the kitchen window.

A couple of minutes later, I heard the door slam.

After six hours in the kitchen, I let Chef Tedis know I was leaving, and I made my way out to the forest. Once I was away from everyone else, I summoned my Dragon and took wing. I flew up and then circled, letting the warm, rising air from the ground keep me aloft as I just enjoyed the feel of the wind on my wings. It seemed like it had been a long time since I'd flown just for the fun of it—since Arden and I had flown to Greenland for a couple of days. It was nice.

I let my course generally head toward where I thought I might find the Elves, my goal being to see whether they'd figured out what the "halo" around me was. I hoped it was the key to unlocking whatever magic had robbed my life from me. I was in no rush, though, content to glide and relax.

So, when I felt a mental tap, a polite sort of mental projection pressure to let me know I wasn't alone, I wasn't thrilled at the interruption to my me-time. I shifted my Mahier-enhanced vision until I found the source—a Woland rising to intercept me. The presence felt familiar, but the Dragon's form was just as familiar, and at the moment, largely unwelcome.

I projected directly, *Cairo. Why are you here?*

I folded my wings back, trading altitude for velocity, and leveled out just above the trees at several hundred miles per hour. Hopefully, my unwelcome company wouldn't be able to keep up, lacking the stored energy my altitude had given me. A glance back showed him trailing farther behind.

Good.

His thought-speak violated my privacy as he projected to me, *I had no idea there was another Keeper of Dragons.*

Startled, I staggered, my flapping awkward, and plummeted twenty feet, nearly hitting a redwood tree. *Wait, what? You can see who I am?*

Your Mahier has a tint to it that's different. Just like Eva's. I know now that you're a Keeper, too. Will you stop? ...Please?

I couldn't get to the ground fast enough. My friend was back! I summoned my human just before talons touched dirt and staggered to a stop. Turning around, I found Cairo landing, as well. He'd managed to catch up—always the better flier of the two of us.

I grinned at him and walked toward him. "I can't believe it. You know who I am! By Aprella, I've dreamed of this. Does Eva know? Can we go see her?"

Cairo held up his hand. "Whoa. Slow down. Who do you

think I am? I'm not taking some stranger to go see Eva until I know more about your intentions. No offense intended, Keeper."

I realized my mouth was open and closed it hard enough to clack my teeth together. I had to force my hands to unclench as I took a deep breath. To have my hopes raised like that... It wasn't fair. Nothing was fair, anymore. I let my breath out slowly, sighing.

"Cairo, you still don't remember me? We were friends, once. And I knew Eva before either of us knew we were Dragons. Tell me you remember me, dammit. Say you know me!"

His gaze was level, and he didn't flinch. He just pursed his lips and almost imperceptibly shook his head.

I didn't much feel like flying, anymore. To be recognized as a Keeper but not as his friend was the opposite of what I would have wished. Yeah, nothing was fair anymore.

CHAPTER 24

Cairo and I walked back to town. Along the way, I told him about when we'd met and all the adventures we'd shared. He recognized enough of the details to believe me, but he still didn't remember me being there. It was frustrating for both of us, I realized, but I was the one with the sense of loss.

At the town entrance, I spotted Arden leaning against the *Welcome to Silver Cove* sign, arms crossed. She waited until we were close to push off from the sign and walk up to us. She had a somber look, though, rather than her usual smile.

"Hello, Arden. Haven't seen you since the last training run. Everything okay?" I gave her a hug, but she returned it only half-heartedly.

"I'm fine. Listen, I had a vision. It just hit me while I was making something to eat and almost knocked me over."

I cocked my head. "You haven't had one of those in a long time. What was it, a warning? Something hopeful, maybe?"

She shook her head. "Better than that. I saw my brother. He was in his room at the Sepens manor. Behind some books in his shelf, he hid a box with small vials in it. Cole... He has the antidote. It'll heal you, and Eva as well. We have to go get it!"

I found myself frowning, though, all the million ways that could go wrong flashing through my head. "No way. Are you kidding? We can't go back to Ochana. You know what's going on there. It's dangerous, even more so for you. What if you get caught? And plus, it's just a vision. That could have been any time, past or future. You don't know it's there right now. You don't even know for sure it's the antidote."

Cairo said, "Seems like a big risk for a maybe."

She ran her fingers through her hair, pushing it out of her eyes, her jaw jutting forward defiantly. "I didn't ask for permission. If we could break the spell on you, Cole, we might be able to do something to stop my father. A chance to make things right. I just wanted to let you know there's hope, and where I'm going. I'm leaving, with or without you, but I do hope you'll come with me. I'm scared, but I'm certain—it's the antidote, and it's in Trey's room."

"You should be scared," I said with more heat than I intended, smoke curling out through my nose. But I already knew my answer, despite my better judgment. "Yeah, I'll come with you. I'm not letting a friend go alone into danger like that."

She flashed a spontaneous smile. "Thank Aprella. If we leave now, we can get there well before dawn. I'm leaving now, anyway. Still coming?"

Cairo grunted. "Sorry to interrupt, but I'm coming, too."

She looked at him as though seeing him for the first time. "Oh? Strength in numbers, sure. I'm surprised, though. You don't even remember him."

"I won't let a Keeper fly without a wingman, especially going someplace as dangerous as Ochana. He's right to be worried. I've seen what it has become. You're not going to like it."

"Regardless, it's something I have to do." She looked back to me. "Let's get going, then. We can feed in Greenland, before flying up.

And just like that, I was headed back to Ochana, the last place in the world I wanted to be.

Getting into Ochana wasn't difficult. Everywhere we looked, I saw Galians and Siens working, closely supervised by red or occasionally green Dragons. And everywhere I looked, the workers were gaunt, often bruised, and all kept their eyes downcast, especially when speaking to those red or green Dragons. The holographic signs and news reports I was accustomed to seeing everywhere, including the huge screens on the Ochana shield, now showed what I can only describe as propaganda. Images of happy Siens working with smiles, or grand looking Wolands protecting Galians from some off-camera danger, interspersed with various formulaic slogans admonishing obedience and diligence for the glory of Ochana.

Although I saw no special markings on the workers that might make us stand out for their absence, we avoided people and kept out of sight as much as possible. Every step we took, I feared some sauntering Woland would challenge us, asking for paperwork authorizing us to wander around unsupervised. When I mentioned that to Cairo, though, he just said that if we were stopped, he'd handle the conversation. He was a Woland, after all. It took longer than I'd have liked to get to the Sepens estate, but Cairo and Arden both agreed with me about taking a cautious route that avoided potential problems.

By the time we saw the wrought iron fence surrounding the manor, dusk had passed. The Sepens manor was dark, and no one moved on the manor grounds.

"What do you think, Arden?" Cairo asked. "Are you still going in there?"

She gazed out at the manor, her lips pursed, and I noticed her foot tapping, her fingers fidgeting. She was nervous, but I couldn't blame her. "Yes, I must. In a way, my father and brother usurping the throne is going to work in our favor since they and the staff aren't here. I assume they're at the castle. Ironic."

He replied, "If they moved to the castle, why would your brother keep anything so valuable here? Wouldn't it be with him, at the castle?"

"My vision was clear. It's here. I recognized the room, the bookshelf, all of it. You guys stay here, okay? Just keep out of sight. I'll sneak in. I can move quieter and faster on my own. I'll just go in, grab it, and then we're out of here. We'll decide when and where to use the antidote after we're safely out of this firestorm. Okay?"

My heart was beating fast, and it felt suddenly warm despite the evening chill. If anything went wrong, there would be little we could do to help her, and the manor was the heart of the enemy, the lion's den. But what choice was there? She had been right about the reward being worth the risk. If I'd needed a reminder why we were doing this, every blue and silver Dragon we'd seen here had been reminder enough.

I nodded. "Okay, Arden. Please be careful. You're the only one who even knows who I am, and I've lost enough friends to Umbran's treachery."

She smiled, though it didn't reach her eyes. "I'll be fine, and soon, so will you. Trust me."

She gave me a hug and then left. I watched her slide through the fence at a point that hadn't looked wide enough, and she made her way lithely through the Sepens grounds. She knew the terrain and moved like a ghost, often passing out of view, though the grounds looked too flat for that. It was kind of impressive, but she'd had lots of practice sneaking in and out, and had come to know every inch of the place. In moments, she was at a barred window, one of the few on the ground floor. She did something to it, and then the bars just swung open like it hadn't been locked at all. She slid the window open, slithered in, and in a heartbeat, she was out of sight.

I played lookout, keeping an eye out for anyone in the area. This was upscale Leslo territory, and neither Cairo nor I exactly fit in.

Cairo said quietly, "Cole, be still. You look suspicious, looking around like that. Just stand with me like we're having a conversation, and be patient."

As nerve-wracking as it was not to look around, I forced myself to stand still, putting my hands in my pockets to help accomplish that monumental feat. I hated waiting, though. Every second was an hour, and I was certain that someone would catch us at any moment. I had no idea how long we'd been waiting, but it felt like an eternity.

A sudden crash of breaking glass from inside made me jump in surprise. A heartbeat later, the interior lights in the manor all came on at once, and through one window on the second story, I saw Arden. And through other windows on every level, more people. Arden turned back toward a door, but two men moved into view, grabbing her. She struggled, but she was no match for the men. They wore Sepens livery.

I charged toward the fence—and ran straight into Cairo's outstretched arm. I tried to get around it, but he grabbed my shirt, then my arm.

"Cole, stop. Look—"

"No! We have to go save her." I pushed at his hand, trying to get free.

Cairo kept his grip and got his other hand on me as well. He pulled me away from the fence, and hard. "There are too many. We have to go. *Now*."

I tried to get free, but he kept me off balance, moving with him by reflex just to stay on my feet. "We can't leave her," I protested.

He ignored my pleas, and as we got to the end of the block, a squad of Wolands emerged onto the street behind us, running through the place we'd been waiting on their way into the manor grounds. If we'd been in there...

I stopped fighting him. It was too late to help Arden. It had been too late the moment those lights went on, but I'd been too focused to realize it. Cairo's interference had kept me from getting captured as well, I realized, but I was too distraught to thank him. We walked in silence through the Leslo neighborhood, into a Galian one, then through Sien apartment buildings. Finally, we reached the market and landing area. He led us north, toward the mountain, to avoid the Woland barracks. We turned west again, and finally reached the ledge.

He didn't slow, just walked right over the edge with me in tow. We dropped about a thousand feet, into a cloud layer, before he shouted to shift. We summoned our Dragons, then headed west over Greenland. I was so upset that it was hard keeping my magic camouflage up, but I managed. We certainly couldn't afford to be spotted by a random patrol wing, though part of me hoped we would so I'd have an excuse to take out my anger on them, even knowing how stupid the fantasy was. There was no way Cairo and I alone could defeat a wing of Dragons.

Only when the east coast of the U.S. came into view did I really come to terms with the fact that we wouldn't be going back, that Arden was gone, and there was nothing we could do about it. We flew in silence, and I was grateful that Cairo didn't comment on the plumes of smoke trailing behind me, the telltale sign of an aggravated Dragon.

We were somewhere over Kentucky by the time I stopped smoking.

Cairo turned his snout to face me, then looked ahead again—then his head whipped back to face me in a blatant double-take. His thought came loud and clear, *Cole... Cole? Wait,* Colton*? Aprella's fangs, where have you been, man?*

I was so surprised when he recognized me—*really* recognized me!—that I nearly fell from the sky.

CHAPTER 25

The sun was well over the horizon behind us when Cairo and I reached Silver Cove. We didn't waste time spiraling down, as was the norm, but dove toward the plaza. As tired as I was from the long flights, transformations, and emotional blow of losing Arden, I nonetheless couldn't contain myself, and didn't bother trying. Instead, I pumped Mahier and Tillium, magically amplifying my Dragon's thought-speech into a kind of mental roar that doubtless echoed in the minds of every person in Silver Cove, urging them to meet at the town square.

As we reached the cobblestone plaza, those who weren't already out and about were hastily staggering outside from their houses. Those who were already out were craning their necks, looking reflexively for the source of that roar.

We touched down moments later and summoned our Human forms, and I sprinted to the water fountain in the plaza center, where I jumped up onto the stone wall. Someone shouted, outraged at being awoken. Others echoed him, but we had a crowd, and it was growing, just like my excitement.

The mayor, Johnathan Maxwell, stepped forward from the crowd. "Cole, is that you? How did you do that, and what's the meaning of this?"

I used magic to carry my voice over the milling residents of Silver Cove, just as I had the alarming bellow. "People of Silver Cove, you know me as Cole Jameson, Sien refugee, but the truth is, I am Prince Colton, Keeper of Dragons, heir to the throne of Ochana—"

"You aren't a Leslo," someone shouted, anger in their voice.

Cairo responded before I could. "Cole speaks the truth. We've all been bespelled, victims of the black magic of Umbran Sepens, and that is why you don't recognize him. But look deep, use your Mahier to see his aura, and you'll see it. You'll see the halo of a Keeper."

I continued, "Umbran Sepens is the rightful king's usurper. King Rylan bends to his will only because his people are under threat. Our brothers and sisters in blue and silver have become Umbran's slaves. Because of him, our noble Wolands enforce Umbran's horrid caste system. He has made their oath twisted, turning them into slave masters. Arden, my friend who came here with me, is Umbran's daughter, though she wishes it were otherwise, and now, he has seized her, taken her as his prisoner. He took one of *us* prisoner. Under Umbran, our people starve. Those who resist are killed or worse. He has separated our families and turned them against us. He has destroyed everything that is good and decent, everything that was Ochana."

Amid a growing chorus of outrage, Johnathan said, "And what are we to do about that? You want to go fight the Red Soldiers? You think you can defeat his Wolands?"

Cairo stepped up onto the wall beside me and shouted, without using Mahier to amplify his voice, "What I think is that it's time to save Ochana. It's time to make our families once again safe. It's past time to make Ochana a healthy place for *all* Dragons, not just the few."

I didn't wait for Johnathan to argue prudence. The time for that had passed. "How many of you have trained with me? Do you think I learned what I taught you by reading a book? I am Prince Cole, son of King Rylan, Keeper of Dragons. I defeated the Time of Fear and slew the dark Elf King. And *I am going to take back Ochana*. I'm going to take back our country and free our families, and I want *all of you* to come with me. I will no longer abide Umbran and his slavery. Now, who is coming with me?"

Cairo raised his fist in the air. "Long live King Rylan! Long live Ochana!"

The crowd surged forward, and through them, my eyes met Johnathan's, and in my head, I dared him to stand in my way.

Instead, though, he nodded to me, his expression grave, and raised his fist as well. "Long live Ochana."

Umbran's reckoning was coming, on leather wings and geysers of flaming Dragonbreath, or I would die trying. I was the Keeper of Dragons in truth once again.

<<<>>>

Keeper of Dragons book 6, Visions of Revolution coming soon!

https://www.jaculican.com/

ABOUT THE AUTHOR

J.A. Culican is a USA Today Bestselling author of the middle grade fantasy series Keeper of Dragons. Her first novel in the fictional series catapulted a trajectory of titles and awards, including top selling author on the USA Today bestsellers list and Amazon, and a rightfully earned spot as an international best seller. Additional accolades include Best Fantasy Book of 2016, Runner-up in Reality Bites Book Awards, and 1st place for Best Coming of Age Book from the Indie Book Awards.

J.A. Culican holds a mAstor's degree in Special Education from Niagara University, in which she has been teaching special education for over 13 years. She is also the president of the autism awareness non-profit Puzzle Peace United. J.A. Culican resides in Southern New Jersey with her husband and four young children.

For more information about J.A. Culican, visit her website at: www.jaculican.com.

ACKNOWLEDGMENTS

Editor: Cassidy Taylor
Cover Designer: Christian Bentulan

www.ingramcontent.com/pod-product-compliance
Lightning Source LLC
Chambersburg PA
CBHW060557310726
48982CB00008B/1155/J

* 9 7 8 1 9 4 9 6 2 1 1 6 7 *